THE KILL LIST

DI SARA RAMSEY #15

M A COMLEY

ACKNOWLEDGMENTS

Special thanks as always go to @studioenp for their superb cover design expertise.

My heartfelt thanks go to my wonderful editor Emmy, my proofreaders Joseph and Barbara for spotting all the lingering nits.

Thank you also to my amazing ARC group who help to keep me sane during this process.

To Mary, gone, but never forgotten. I hope you found the peace you were searching for my dear friend.

ALSO BY M A COMLEY

Unfair Justice (a 10,000 word short story)

Irrational Justice (a 10,000 word short story)

Seeking Justice (a 15,000 word novella)

Caring For Justice (a 24,000 word novella)

Savage Justice (a 17,000 word novella Featuring THE UNICORN)

Gone In Seconds (Justice Again series #1)

Ultimate Dilemma (Justice Again series #2)

Shot of Silence (Justice Again #3)

Taste of Fury (Justice Again #4)

Crying Shame (Justice Again #5)

To Die For (DI Sam Cobbs #1) Coming Dec 2021

Clever Deception (co-written by Linda S Prather)

Tragic Deception (co-written by Linda S Prather)

Sinful Deception (co-written by Linda S Prather)

Forever Watching You (DI Miranda Carr thriller)

Wrong Place (DI Sally Parker thriller #1)

No Hiding Place (DI Sally Parker thriller #2)

Cold Case (DI Sally Parker thriller#3)

Deadly Encounter (DI Sally Parker thriller #4)

Lost Innocence (DI Sally Parker thriller #5)

Goodbye, My Precious Child (DI Sally Parker #6)

The Missing Wife (DI Sally Parker #7) Out Feb 2022)

Web of Deceit (DI Sally Parker Novella with Tara Lyons)

The Missing Children (DI Kayli Bright #1)

Killer On The Run (DI Kayli Bright #2)

Hidden Agenda (DI Kayli Bright #3)

Murderous Betrayal (Kayli Bright #4)

Dying Breath (Kayli Bright #5)

Taken (Kayli Bright #6 coming March 2020)

The Hostage Takers (DI Kayli Bright Novella)

No Right to Kill (DI Sara Ramsey #1)

Killer Blow (DI Sara Ramsey #2)

The Dead Can't Speak (DI Sara Ramsey #3)

Deluded (DI Sara Ramsey #4)

The Murder Pact (DI Sara Ramsey #5)

Twisted Revenge (DI Sara Ramsey #6)

The Lies She Told (DI Sara Ramsey #7)

For The Love Of… (DI Sara Ramsey #8)

Run For Your Life (DI Sara Ramsey #9)

Cold Mercy (DI Sara Ramsey #10)

Sign of Evil (DI Sara Ramsey #11)

Indefensible (DI Sara Ramsey #12)

Locked Away (DI Sara Ramsey #13)

I Can See You (DI Sara Ramsey #14)

The Kill List (DI Sara Ramsey #15) coming March 2022

I Know The Truth (A psychological thriller)

She's Gone (A psychological thriller)

The Caller (co-written with Tara Lyons)

Evil In Disguise – a novel based on True events

Deadly Act (Hero series novella)

Torn Apart (Hero series #1)

End Result (Hero series #2)

In Plain Sight (Hero Series #3)

Double Jeopardy (Hero Series #4)

Criminal Actions (Hero Series #5)

Regrets Mean Nothing (Hero #6)

PROLOGUE

*T*he nights were getting lighter by the day, thankfully. Kelly's pace quickened. She had a date to look forward to this evening. Her stomach had been tied in knots for most of the afternoon at the thought of what lay ahead of her. She'd been keen on Jackson for a few months, he was the doctor she had worked alongside for a while now. Everything appeared to be going her way for a change. The estate agent had put her flat on the market the week before and achieved the full market price within the first couple of viewings, sending her head in a spin. Now all she had to do was put a deposit down at the weekend on the new-build she'd had her eye on, which was situated out in the country, and her life would be sorted, finally going in the right direction.

She needed a break. Life over the last couple of years had knocked her sideways. First, her father had died of a heart attack at the age of fifty-four. His death had been totally unexpected, and her fiancé at the time, Matt, had ditched her not long after. His excuse? Her doom-and-gloom attitude was making his life unbearable and he was sick of her moods bringing him down. How dare he be so selfish? She'd just lost her father, for fuck's sake, what did he expect her to do? Leap up and down, rejoicing in the fact her father had gone to his grave at such an early age?

Kelly shook her head, dislodging Matt's angry features. *I'm well shot of that arsehole.* Crossing the next corner, she smiled as Jackson's handsome face entered her mind. It had taken him a while to pluck up the courage to ask her out; he had always come across as quite shy in comparison to Matt. She hadn't hesitated in accepting when he'd asked her for a date. He'd seen her to the door of the hospital one night, pretending he needed some fresh air. She thought it odd at the time, never dreaming what he had on his mind.

That had happened last week, and she'd been light-footed and had a few sleepless nights ever since their first date which had taken place at one of her favourite restaurants, Miller and Carter, and now there was yet another date about to happen and the butterflies were already fluttering furiously. She upped her pace; the block of flats she'd soon be leaving lay just around the corner. Kelly detested the place now that she had sold it, couldn't wait to move on, wished she was moving out next week instead of having to wait a couple of months for the sale to go through the system. She had never really fallen in love with the flat since the day she'd moved in a couple of years before. Why she had bothered to buy the property in the first place had always been a major mystery. Her parents had tried their best to dissuade her, but she'd dug her heels in, refusing to listen to their point of view—she had seen their objections as them still trying to rule her life, and she needed a break from all that.

The lift took her up to her floor. She screwed her nose up at the new patch of graffiti some kind soul had scribbled along the balcony, thankful that it had happened this week rather than a couple of weeks before when her buyer had shown interest in her flat. *Pigs. Why do these Neanderthals insist on spoiling their environment? Utter disgrace, that's what it is. I'll be glad to get out of here, it can't come soon enough.*

She travelled the length of the balcony, admiring the view of the River Wye. That would be the only downside to moving out, she would no longer have such a wondrous view. However, there were too many positives to her move to consider, and she'd focus on them over the coming weeks, once she'd put the deposit down on the new house. It would mean she'd need to move back home with her mother for a few months until the new property was built, but c'est la vie!

Kelly removed her key from her pocket and paused. The door was ajar. She tried to cast her mind back to that morning. She'd been running late for her shift at the hospital. Had she forgotten to close the door in her rush to get there? She didn't think so. *Shit! What do I do now? What if there's a burglar inside?* She glanced back at the graffiti. What if the person who had scribbled that obscenity had found their way into her flat? There was no one around—had there have been, she would have asked them to accompany her into the flat, just to check everything was all right.

Nope, she was on her own. Easing open the front door, she strained an ear but heard nothing. No sign of anyone wrecking the place, not from what she could tell. She inched farther into the flat, leaving the front door open in case she had to make a swift exit. "Hello, is anybody here?" she cried out tentatively. *Would a burglar respond? Silly cow, what was I thinking?*

Kelly ventured into the lounge to find a man dressed in a suit, sitting on the sofa. "Excuse me? What the hell do you think you're doing in my flat?"

"Take a seat, Kelly."

"Do I know you? What do you want?"

He smiled and gestured for her to sit opposite him. "I said, take a seat. Now do it!"

"Like fuck I will. What gives you the right to break into my home and tell me what to do? Who are you?" She'd never been the type to try and bargain with someone if she was vexed. She stood rooted to the spot and crossed her arms in defiance. "You can't order me around. Tell me who you are and what you're doing here. You've got two seconds or I'm calling the police."

The man laughed then stopped and glared at her. "If I tell you to fucking do something, you'll do it. This is your last chance. Sit. Down."

Fear tapped at her bones. His voice had a menacing edge to it. She was in a quandary over what to do next, but then the decision was removed from her hands instantly with a whack to the head from behind. She stumbled forward, lost her footing and landed at the man's feet.

He leaned forward and grabbed her uniform at the neck. "When I tell you to do something, I expect you to do it. Am I making myself clear, whore?"

Her throat constricted, preventing her from responding. She nodded instead and tried to look behind her, but his hand tightened, stopping her from moving. There was obviously someone else in the room, but who? She tried to speak; her words came out as a whisper. "What do you want from me?"

"You've been a naughty girl. We're here to punish you."

Thinking he had got the wrong person, she opened her mouth to object.

He shook his head. "Keep your mouth shut and listen."

She nodded. *I'll do anything you ask, if you'll please leave me alone. I don't want to get hurt.*

"As I said, we're here to punish you for the sins you have committed."

"What? I don't know what you're talking about. You've got the wrong person. Please, let me go," she snivelled.

"You're wrong. Kelly Pittman." He grinned and tilted his head. "See, I know your name, I'm aware that I have the right flat, so stop complaining."

"Why? What have I done to you?"

He raised an eyebrow. "You've done nothing to me. But you've done plenty to a friend of mine. Now he wants retribution, and you know what?"

She shook her head, shock taking over.

"He's going to get it."

"Get on with it," a female voice said from behind Kelly.

She tried to see who the person was, but his hand tightened on her uniform again, restricting her movements.

4

"Seriously, I haven't got a clue what you're talking about," Kelly whimpered. "Please, I think you're making a grave mistake."

He sneered. "Not! We know who you are and what you're guilty of. You'll go to your maker today, knowing that you could have prevented this outcome, if only you had made the right decision a few months back."

She frowned and cast her mind back. *What does he mean? Has this got something to do with my father's death? With me breaking up with Matt? They're the only two instances I can think of that occurred a few months ago. Neither of them would warrant someone coming here to end my life. What the actual fuck!* "I have no idea what you're talking about. You've made a mistake, and now I want you to leave my home." Her voice and courage sounded a little shaky, even to her own ears. "Is this something to do with Matt?"

"It might be. Anyway, I've had enough of all this chatting, we have places to go and people to see, so let's get on with things. Get up." He rose to his feet and hoisted her off the floor to stand.

"What are you going to do to me? I've done nothing wrong. You've made a huge mistake. Please don't do this."

His forehead touched hers. "I won't tell you again, shut the fuck up."

"I'm getting bored with you having a conversation with this bimbo. Let's get on with it and get out of here," the woman behind urged.

Kelly was at a loss to know what to do, however, she knew she had to go down fighting, it wasn't in her not to. She caught the man off-guard, clenched her fist and belted him across the face.

"Why, you fucking bitch. I'll make you sorry you did that." He punched her several times in the stomach, winding her.

Kelly's legs gave way beneath her. He released the hand he was holding her up with, letting her drop to the floor, and then kicked her a few times, in the lower back and her legs.

"Stop it. Please, no more. I'll do anything you want me to do."

He paused mid-kick and looked over at the young woman who Kelly could now see for the first time. She tried to recall if she'd seen either one of them before and came up blank. She offered up one more plea, aware that it would probably fall on deaf ears. "Please, don't do this."

The girl stepped forward and lashed out at her, striking her face over and over until Kelly ducked out of the way. All of this was making no sense to Kelly at all, and she could see no way out of the situation.

The man caught hold of the woman's arm, restraining her. "We don't have time for this. Let's get the deed done and get out of here."

"I agree."

Kelly glanced up to see them both advancing towards her again. She scurried across the room on her hands and knees but couldn't escape them. They grabbed each of her arms and yanked her onto her feet. She glanced at the man and then the woman and tried to tug her arms from their grasps. "Don't do this. I have money set aside for a new house. I can give it to you, if you'll leave me alone."

"You think this is about money?" the man sneered.

"I don't know what this is about. I truly believe you have the wrong person. I'm a simple nurse. My main aim in life is to make people feel better. I've never knowingly hurt anyone before. Please, tell me what I'm supposed to have done and I'll endeavour to put things right ASAP."

"It's too late for that now. You and the others put the nails in the coffin and now you need to be punished."

"You keep saying that, but I'm telling you, you've got this all wrong. At least tell me what I'm supposed to have done wrong. Please, I'm begging you. On my mother's life, I haven't knowingly harmed anyone."

The couple remained silent and guided her to the far wall. The wall made of glass, overlooking the beautiful River Wye. Fear ripped at her insides. The woman opened the patio door, and the three of them walked out onto the six-foot-wide balcony. The evening sun warmed her face.

"Please, what are you going to do to me?" She thought about screaming but had a feeling that would only anger them more. She needed to try to talk them round.

"You'll find out soon enough. Hold both of her arms and I'll grab her legs," the man instructed.

The woman clasped both of her wrists in her hands, and Kelly found herself being lifted off the floor by the man.

"No!" she finally screamed out. The tears fell then, and her heart rate was intense, beating erratically, so fast she thought it was going to tear through her chest like an express train.

Between them, they hoisted her over the balcony, and then she was in mid-air, hurtling towards the ground. She screamed louder than she'd ever screamed before, but what was the point? Thoughts of leaving her mother behind was all she managed to think about before she hit the pavement at speed.

1

---

*D*etective Inspector Sara Ramsey and her partner, Detective
Sergeant Carla Jameson, had just ended their shift for the
day and were on their way out of the station. The desk sergeant, Jeff,
was on the phone. He raised his finger, instructing them to wait and,
after a moment or two, ended his call.

"What's up, Jeff?" Sara asked.

"No, it's okay. You get off, my guys can deal with it."

"Deal with what?" Sara insisted.

"Yeah, go on. You've got us intrigued now," Carla chipped in.

"Well, I've just received a call about a fatal accident in the centre
of town. At the block of flats down by the river."

Sara heard where the location was and her heart lurched against her
ribs. "And? What happened?"

"A young woman fell from one of the top flats."

"Shit! Fell or was she pushed?" Sara dared to ask, her mind already
switched on to the case.

"That's the sixty-four-million-dollar question," he replied. "It's
okay, we'll deal with it."

Sara looked at her partner. "Shall we take a drive over there and
have a butcher's?"

Carla rolled her eyes. "Like I have an option."

Sara grinned. "We'd better take both cars, then we can go our separate ways afterwards."

"Okay by me."

"I guess we'll see you in the morning, Jeff."

"You will that, ma'am. Have a good evening, when you finally knock off duty, that is."

Sara pushed open the door and called over her shoulder, "You, too."

Outside, she and Carla jumped into their respective cars. The first thing Sara did was call her husband. "Hi, Mark, are you home yet?"

"I was just leaving the surgery. Do you need me to pick something up on the way home?"

"No, I think we're all right for supplies from what I can remember. Umm… Carla and I were just leaving the station when we got the call that there has been a fatal accident in town. We're on our way over there now to check it out."

"Oh my. Do you know what happened?"

"Not really, except a woman has fallen to her death from a block of flats."

Mark paused for a second or two and then replied, "Ouch. Not the same block of flats where Tim died, is it?"

"The very same. I know where this is leading, I'm fine, don't worry about me. I can't avoid the place for the rest of my life. It's just not in me to do that, love. Anyway, I have to shoot now. I'll try not to be too long."

"As long as you're sure. Any preference for dinner tonight?"

"I haven't given it much thought, sorry."

"No need to apologise, leave it with me, I'll surprise you. Something quick but nourishing, how does that sound?"

"Perfect. I love you, Mark."

"I know. It's a good job the feeling is mutual. Take care, see you later."

She ended the call and gave Carla the thumbs-up, noting that her partner had been watching her with her lips still, so she couldn't have called home to speak to Des. *Maybe he's still at work.*

Sara parked behind the familiar van, belonging to the female pathologist in the area. Lorraine's shocking red hair acted like a beacon for her and Carla to follow.

"Should we suit up?" Carla asked.

"Yep, I think we should, rather than get a bollocking from Lorraine for being shoddy. I've got a couple of suits in the boot." After handing Carla a protective suit, they both popped them on, covered their shoes with the blue plastic slip-ons and set off to join Lorraine.

"What are you two doing here?" Lorraine asked, surprised to see them.

"We thought we'd drop by and have a gander. What have we got, apart from the obvious?" Sara asked, staring down at the bloody and twisted body of a female splayed on the concrete at her feet.

Lorraine tutted. "My initial examination is pointing to a suspicious death."

Sara frowned and glanced at her pathologist friend. "How can you tell?"

"By the injuries she has on her body. I don't believe they're due to the fall at all."

"She put up a fight before she fell, is that what you're telling us?"

"Or tried to, unsuccessfully by the look of things."

Sara's gaze travelled the height of the building. "How far did she fall, do you know?"

"One of her neighbours informed us that she lived on the fourteenth floor at number two hundred and twenty-five."

"Is the neighbour around?"

"No. She was in shock, so I sent her back to her flat and told her someone from the police would be visiting her soon to take a statement. She lives in the flat on the right."

Sara nodded. "We'll do that." She cast an apologetic glance Carla's way. Her partner shrugged, letting her know that she'd expected it. "Was she the one who found the body? Who called nine-nine-nine?"

"That's right. I didn't get much out of her apart from the fact that the victim's first name was Kelly and that she was a nurse."

"Shit! Always ticks me off when I hear of someone in the medical profession losing their life. Anything else for us?"

Lorraine's gaze drifted to the sky. "Nope, we're going to have to get a move on, covering the body before that black cloud heads our way."

"Okay, in other words, piss off and leave you to it." Sara grinned.

"I keep telling you what a wise lady you are."

"One of these days I'll start believing you. We'll drop back and see you before we leave."

Lorraine gave a brief nod and then turned her attention to the SOCO techs in the nearest vicinity. "Let's get the tent up, lads. Quick smart."

Sara and Carla took off their protective suits and shoved them in the black bag close to the cordon. Then they made their way over to the lift and rode it to the fourteenth floor. Sara's stomach contorted itself into several knots.

Carla picked up on her reluctance as they took a step out of the lift. "Are you sure you're up to this?"

Sara smiled and batted away the suggestion with a floppy hand. "Not really, but needs must. I'll be fine, once we're out of here."

"Go home and leave the interviewing to me on this one."

"I wouldn't dream of it."

"What you mean is that you don't trust me," Carla grumbled.

Sara stopped walking and clawed at Carla's arm. "That's a load of bollocks and you damn well know it, Carla Jameson."

Her partner smiled broadly. "Yeah, I know. But I like to play the martyr now and again to keep you on your toes."

Sara smiled and shook her head. "Sometimes, just *sometimes*, I could willingly give you a good slap."

Carla placed a hand over her chest and gasped. "And risk being pulled over the coals by HQ on an assault charge?"

"You wouldn't!"

Carla shrugged. "Ditto. Which flat was it again?"

Sara stared ahead of her, along the concrete balcony. "Three doors down is the victim's flat, we'll see what we can gather there first."

"Without suits on?"

"Nope, I didn't say we'd go in, not unless someone is in there with a couple of spare suits for us." They walked towards the open doorway, and Sara called out. "Anybody here?"

A rustling SOCO tech came to the doorway which had been cordoned off with crime scene tape. "Yep, we're here. You can't come in here, not without the right gear on."

"I'm well aware of procedures, thanks all the same." Sara offered up a tight grin for the young tech.

He mumbled an apology. "Sorry, I've not been on the job long and, so far, I've had several officers disregarding my instructions, which in turn has got me into bother with the pathologist."

"Sorry to hear that. You're going to need to stand your ground firmer in the future."

He nodded. "That's what Lorraine advised me to do. Easier said than done with some coppers."

"I hear you. I don't suppose you've got a spare suit for each of us, have you? We used the ones we had with us downstairs to assess the crime scene."

He smiled and raised a finger. "Wait there, I have a couple in my bag."

"You're a star."

The tech raced down the small hallway and emerged a few moments later carrying two packets containing white suits and shoe covers for them.

"Here we go again," Sara said, slipping into one of the suits and zipping up the front.

Carla did the same, then the tech detached one side of the tape to allow them to enter the flat. They signed the Crime Scene Log and then followed him into the lounge at the rear. Sara's gaze was immediately drawn to the open patio door that led out onto the balcony overlooking the River Wye. Her heart lurched again, when confronted with the view that looked so familiar; it had been the same vista from her brother's flat.

"That's where it happened, I mean, she went down from there," the tech said, stating the obvious.

Sara took a few steps towards the balcony but stopped to examine an area on the carpet before she reached the patio doors. "Several areas of blood, some heavier than others, I see."

"That's right. I believe it was likely someone attacked her. Maybe she brought someone home with her and he tried it on, he then got arsy with her, and she got bashed for not complying with his wishes."

Sara smiled at the young man. "You have a pretty vivid imagination there."

He shrugged. "Maybe. It's possible, though."

"It's one scenario we can latch on to. We never like to rule out anything at this early stage."

"My take is, she was beaten up here, maybe knocked unconscious, and then probably tipped over the balcony. What a way to go. Horrendous, right?" the tech suggested.

Tutting and sighing, Sara had to agree with his assumption. "The only problem is that she was heard screaming, wasn't she?"

"Ah, maybe she woke up halfway down," the tech blurted out, without needing to consider his response first.

"Either way, she was tossed off the balcony, that much is evident, so we'll be noting this one down as a murder inquiry. Anything else here we should be concerned about?"

He shook his head, and they all glanced around the room at the markers laid out at various points on the carpet.

"I don't think so. I haven't had a chance to take a look elsewhere in the flat yet. I mean, I've had a brief peek into the bathroom and the bedroom, but there doesn't seem to be anything out of the ordinary going on in either room. I concluded this is where the struggle took place."

"Good job. Mind if we take a brief look ourselves?" Sara asked.

"Not at all. The bathroom is off to the left and the bedroom is back up the hallway on the right."

"Thanks, what about the kitchen?"

"Next to the bathroom. Nothing in there either, as far as I can tell."

Sara took a few paces to her right and poked her head into what could only be described as a kitchenette. There were no telltale signs on the worktop, it was clear. No stray mugs or glasses in sight, which was a telling sign for Sara. It meant that whoever had entered the flat hadn't stuck around for long to visit the victim.

She moved on to the bedroom to find it contained a white wardrobe and matching chest of drawers and two bedside tables next to a double bed, the bedding of which remained tidy and undisturbed. Another indication that the visitor hadn't stayed around for long. "Was it a chance encounter gone wrong?" she muttered.

Carla was standing right behind her, peering over her shoulder. "Maybe. We won't know until we've spoken to any possible witnesses or family members."

"Yep. We need to find out her full name before we can start tracing her family."

"I'll call the station, see what they can find out."

Sara squeezed past her partner and returned to the lounge. "You were right, nothing in either of the rooms to warrant further investigation. Any forms of ID anywhere?" Her gaze darted around the room and zeroed in on a woman's handbag on one of the chairs closest to the door. "May I?"

"Go for it. Wait, I'll get you some gloves." He rushed over to his tech case and returned with a pair of blue gloves and handed them to Sara.

"Thanks. I usually carry a set in my pocket but forgot to renew the last ones I used." She picked up the shoulder bag. It had an extra-long strap, the type that crossed the body for added security, telling her that the victim was usually a cautious person. *So how had this happened to her?* "Right, what do we have here? Her bank card says Miss K E Pittman. So that will do for me. We've also got her hospital ID here. She was an Accident and Emergency nurse at Hereford Hospital."

"Blast. That's a shame," the tech said, his chin sinking onto his chest in remorse.

"We knew she was a nurse, Lorraine told us as much downstairs. But maybe there's a lead we can follow if she's an A and E nurse."

"Possibly," Carla stated, reappearing from the hallway. "I overheard you've located her handbag. The station confirmed her surname."

Sara continued to search the handbag and discovered the victim's mobile. "This should give us her family's numbers, if we can get into it." She attempted the usual numbers they always tried when they found a mobile: four zeros and two-four-six-eight, but without success. "Nope, not this time." She rummaged in the bag some more and found a small notebook. Flicking through it, all she found was what appeared to be friend's numbers and addresses, no family members for some reason. "We'll see if the neighbour has a contact number for us. I think we're done here. Thanks for all your help." Sara smiled at the tech.

"You're welcome. I hope your investigation runs smoothly and without hitches."

Sara winced. "Thanks for jinxing it."

He cringed and chewed on his bottom lip. "Sorry."

Sara sniggered. "I was kidding. See you again soon, no doubt. And remember what I said about not taking any shit from my colleagues. Stand your ground and you'll do okay."

"Thanks, I appreciate your advice."

Sara and Carla left the flat and went next door. Sara used the knocker to gain the homeowner's attention.

A woman in her early fifties opened the door and brushed back her shoulder-length hair with a shaking hand. "Hello, I've been expecting you."

Sara smiled, trying to put her at ease. The woman seemed anxious. "I'm DI Sara Ramsey, and this is my partner, DS Carla Jameson. Is it all right if we come in and have a chat with you?"

"Yes, of course."

Sara smiled. "We'll just slip off our protective gear first." The rustling commenced and ended when Sara and Carla placed the suits in the black bag by the front door of the victim's flat.

The woman took a step back. "I'm Audrey Cotton by the way."

"Thanks for agreeing to see us, Mrs Cotton."

"Nonsense, and please, call me Audrey, it's more informal. Can I get you a drink?"

Sara held up her hand. "We'll decline if it's all the same to you."

"No problem. Come through to the lounge, I've got the gas fire on and it's warmer in there."

The lounge was a cosy affair. Several shelves adorned the walls and they were cluttered with various knick-knacks, anything from ornaments to small picture frames of the woman with different members of her family, or so Sara presumed.

"Please, take a seat." Audrey gestured for them both to sit on the sofa while she sat in the armchair close to the blazing fire. "Not too warm in here for you, is it?"

"Not at all. It's the warmest I've felt all day. Rather chilly for March at the moment, isn't it?"

"It is that. Still, we mustn't grumble, not after the bleak winter we've just survived, well, some of us." She shook her head, and her gaze dipped to the carpet in front of her. "Poor Kelly, such a sweet girl. How something like that could happen to her, I'll never know." She ran a hand over her face.

"Did you know her well?"

"I suppose you could say that. She used to give me some extra groceries. We sort of shared things, like half a loaf of bread, or some veggies, it's better than wasting the produce when you live on your own. I repaid her, of course. We made a list most weeks, essentials we both needed, and then split them in two."

"That was nice. Makes sense rather than throw the stuff away," Sara agreed.

"That's right. I'm devastated she's no longer with us. Do you know what happened to her? I mean, it's not like her balcony was that low that she would mistakenly tumble over the top. So someone must have pushed her, or is that me talking out of my arse? I watch a lot of crime shows on TV, therefore I have a very suspicious mind. Very little trust nowadays. Not a bad thing, it keeps me out of trouble."

"Am I to understand that you were the one to discover the body?"

"Yes, I'd nipped out to the chippy. Of course, after coming back and seeing her like that... dead, my tea went straight in the bin. Couldn't stand the thought of eating it, not after being confronted with her dead body." She shuddered.

"I quite understand. So you didn't hear any form of commotion going on in the flat next door before Kelly died then?"

"No. I'd been out since five-thirty. There was a blasted long queue in the chippy, and the bloke before me, I think he must have been feeding a bloody football team, the amount he was ordering. I had to hang around while they put a second and then a third batch of chips in the fryer. Wish I hadn't bothered now, especially as it all ended up in the bin anyway. Sorry, I shouldn't say that, not when that poor girl has lost her life this evening."

"Kelly was still in her uniform. Can you tell me at what time she usually finished work in the evening? Or did she work the night shift and was due to begin her shift soon?"

"No, she always worked the day shift, started around eight or nine, not sure when exactly, and worked until around six or seven every night."

"We'll check with the hospital to get an accurate time for when her shift ended today."

"Yes, that's a good idea." Audrey shook her head over and over again. "Why would someone do that to her? I'm still struggling to comprehend that much. What a vile world we live in. Isn't the pandemic killing off enough people as it is? Why do people have to go out of their way to add to the death toll? And not only that, it's yet another woman who has lost her life. I dread to think how many that has been in Hereford this year. I'm old enough to remember when it used to be safe for women to venture out and walk the streets alone, not nowadays. Oh God, I'm off."

"Except Kelly wasn't walking the streets, was she? She was at home when the incident occurred."

"Yes, you're right. I stand corrected. My hubby used to tell me I talked a lot of shit at times."

Sara waited while the woman fell quiet as if she was reliving the time she had with her husband. "Has he been gone long?"

"Three years next month, not that I'm counting." She smiled, her eyes glistening with tears.

"I'm sorry for your loss."

Audrey's gaze connected with Sara's. "I'm not, not really. He was a grade-A tosser nine-tenths of the time. Abusive, verbally and physically, until the day I fought back and bopped him one on the nose, broke the damn thing. He changed his ways then. Men enjoy pushing the boundaries, bullying women. If more women fought back, I bet most men would run a mile, probably home to their mothers."

"You might be right there." Sara chuckled and then winced and glanced sideways at Carla, suddenly recalling her partner had lived through a life of hell with her former boyfriend, Gary.

Carla sensed she was looking at her, glanced up from her notebook, smiled briefly and dropped her head once more.

Sara turned her attention back to Audrey again and asked, "Did Kelly live alone?"

"Oh, yes. She wasn't really one for male company, if you know what I mean?"

Sara inclined her head and asked, "Was she gay?"

"Good heavens, I didn't mean *that*." Audrey paused and then shook her head. "The thought never crossed my mind. No, what I meant was that she didn't have many male friends calling, not like some of the residents around here. The girl three doors down seems to have at least three different male callers every week, from what I can tell. Not that I'm out there snooping around every minute of the day. Oh dear, I seem to be digging myself into a hole here."

Sara smiled. "You're not. You've suffered a severe shock to the system. Try and take a few calming breaths. Can I get you a cup of tea perhaps?"

Audrey waved a finger. "No, that won't be necessary, you're far too busy to pamper me. Now, where were we? Ah, yes, I think Kelly's last boyfriend was a few months ago. It was a brief affair, she complained that she found out he was using her just to get his feet under the table because he was being evicted from the flat he was renting. Bloody men, there always seems to be something going on in their heads, they can never treat a woman how they expect to be treated, can they?"

Sara chewed on her bottom lip, suppressing her reply for a moment. "Actually, I have a gem of a husband. We're very much equal in our relationship." She turned to face Carla. "You're in a minority, too, Carla, aren't you?"

"Thankfully, with my current beau, yes." Carla beamed and then got back to making her notes.

"That's good to hear, ladies. It must be really tough having excellent relationships when you're both busy working women."

"Sometimes. We both have understanding partners, so that helps. I don't suppose you can recall the name of Kelly's last boyfriend, can you?"

Audrey placed a finger and thumb either side of her chin as she thought. "Now then, what was it? Maurice, Mark...? No, it was Matt. Please don't go expecting me to give you his surname, I couldn't possibly remember that. Again, not much use, am I?"

"Something is better than nothing. Any idea where he worked?"

"That's easy, I believe the term is he was between jobs. Another reason why Kelly lost patience with him. He used to come round, treat her like a slave, expecting her to wait on him without bloody putting his hand in his pocket. She confided in me that she didn't have it in her to end the relationship. I brought her in here and told her a few home truths. Listened to her woes and concerns and then pointed out that all he was doing was using her. At first, she thought I was being a bitch, but I ended up planting the seed if you will, and I think her suspicions grew from there. A few weeks later she gave him the boot." She smiled and sighed while she caught her breath. "I have to tell you, within days, the old Kelly was back. Happy-go-lucky, smiling every time I saw her. She revelled in her freedom to come and go as she pleased once more. Why do men treat women so badly? Or more to the point, why in God's name do younger women allow men to treat them so cruelly?"

"It sounds like Kelly realised her mistake before things went too far, thanks to your intervention. Sometimes it takes an outsider to point out the failings in our relationships, doesn't it?"

Audrey nodded. "I think that's spot on. Anyway, what I'm trying to say is that Kelly was happy and settled in her life. She adored being a nurse, even during the pandemic, when she came home dead on her feet most days. She always had a smile pinned on that pretty face of hers. I shall miss her terribly."

"What about family? Does she have anyone in the area?"

"Oh, yes, she was a local lass. Although, she let it slip once that she had a fairly distant relationship with her mother because of her alcoholism."

"Her mother's?"

"That's right. The only time she really contacted Kelly with the pretence she cared about her was when she was short of cash to buy her next bottle of vodka. So, after she confided in me, I suppose I felt obliged to take her under my wing. I treated her like the daughter I never had, you see. That's why this has all come as a huge shock to me."

"You're a wonderful person, Mrs Cotton. There are not many around like you, not these days."

"I do my best. It doesn't take much to shower someone with kindness, especially if they have a heart of gold, like Kelly. At the risk of repeating myself, I will miss her dreadfully. I just hope the person who replaces her next door is just as nice."

"That's always a concern, living in a block of flats like this. Sorry, going back to Kelly's mother, I don't suppose you have her address, do you?"

She smiled and reached down and lifted her handbag. After unzipping it, she searched the interior, cussing now and then when something evaded her. "Where is it? Where did I put the damn thing?" She glanced at the table in the corner and tutted. "Silly me, I had it out the other day while I parcelled up my sister's birthday present." She left her chair to collect a small notebook. "Now where is it? Ah, here it is. Oh God, her mother is going to be devastated."

"I thought you said they didn't get along," Sara said.

"Maybe I exaggerated a bit. Her father died three or four months ago, that's why her mother turned to drink. She found it impossible to cope without him. She even pleaded with Kelly to move back home to be with her, rather than be lonely. Kelly had a huge dilemma on her hands for a few weeks, not wanting to let her mother down, but one day she went round there and her mother was rat-arsed, I think that's the correct term. Well, she started hurling ornaments at Kelly, and anything else she could lay her hands on. It was enough to send the poor girl scampering back home. I heard her breaking her heart through the walls and went round there to see if I could help. When she told me what had happened, I felt so sorry for Kelly, she didn't deserve to be treated like that, not by her own mother. I hugged her, cradled her in my arms and rocked her back and forth while she sobbed for a good few hours. She'd just lost her father, she was in bits, and then seeing her mother like that, well, it tainted their relationship overnight really. It would do, wouldn't it? I know if my mother ever treated me that way, she wouldn't see hide nor hair of me ever again. Who needs that type of stress or aggro in their lives? She didn't, not after working her butt off to save peoples' lives at the height of the pandemic. All I can say is her mother is a selfish bitch and now I suppose you'll be going round there to break the unwanted news to her about Kelly. I dread to think how she'll react, you know, after grieving for her husband for the past few months—if she has been grieving for him, I have my doubts. Maybe that's me being harsh. Sorry, I'll shut up now, I've chuntered on enough."

"It's okay, it's the shock talking."

"I suppose it is. I've got the image of her twisted body lying on the ground running through my mind. I can't seem to shake it off. That poor, poor young lady. May she rest in peace."

Sara's heart went out to the woman who had obviously cared very deeply about the victim, however, they had a job to do, and it was important to get on with the investigation. "Sorry to rush you, you were about to give us Kelly's mother's address."

"So I was. Silly me. Her name is Patricia Pittman, and she lives at sixty-two Hawk's Avenue out in Tupsley. It's close to the main road so should be easy to find, from what I could gather from Kelly."

"Thanks, that's a great help. Is there anything else you can tell us that you believe might help our investigation?"

She returned to her seat and let out a large sigh. "I don't think so. Who do you think did this? I know it's a ridiculous question at this stage, but what I suppose I'm asking is, whether I should feel concerned for my own safety. I know that probably sounds very selfish of me."

"It doesn't. It sounds logical. All I can tell you is that there will be sufficient police and SOCO presence here for the next few days, so that should ease any concerns you may have. Maybe it would be better if you found alternative accommodation for a week or so, if you feel that apprehensive."

Audrey nodded. "Yes, I might just do that, go to my sister's down in Devon. She's always hounding me about visiting her, so this would be an ideal opportunity."

"I agree. Maybe you could give us your mobile number, just in case we have any further questions for you while you're away."

"Is that likely?"

"Possibly, it depends on what we uncover in the meantime."

She reeled off the number, and Carla noted it down.

Then Sara stood and announced their departure. "I can't thank you enough for taking the time to speak to us at this sad time. We really appreciate all the information you've given us."

"It was nothing. I hope you find the person responsible and punish them properly. You hear of so many cases where the criminals get off lightly these days. Please, don't let this case be one of those."

"We're going to do our absolute best, I can assure you. Stay there, we'll see ourselves out."

"If you're sure?"

Sara smiled and waved goodbye to the distraught woman. Carla followed her up the hallway and out of the front door.

"That was tough, she obviously cared deeply for Kelly," Carla stated.

"Yes, very sad, after her own mother let her down so badly."

"Grief affects everyone differently. I seem to recall a very wise woman telling me that recently."

"I did, didn't I? I stand by that statement, too. Let's knock on a few more doors, see if anyone either saw or heard anything, if not, we'll leave uniform to carry out the house-to-house enquiries for us while we go and break the news to Kelly's mother."

"Good idea. Do you want to split up?"

"Makes sense. I'll try the neighbour on the other side and you take the flat next door."

Sara knocked on the door and a young man in his late twenties opened it. He looked her up and down and asked, "Can I help?"

She produced her warrant card and thrust it in his face. "We're investigating a crime that has been committed and wondered if you could shed any light on it."

"What crime? I haven't done anything. How dare you come to my door accusing me?"

Sara raised her hands to stop him mouthing off. "I didn't say you had. Your neighbour was found downstairs. Apparently, she fell from her balcony earlier this evening. I just wondered if you'd either heard or had seen anything out of the ordinary today."

"Crap. I heard a scream earlier but didn't think anything of it."

"Did that come from inside or outside the flat, possibly as she fell?"

"How the heck should I know? It would take some doing to fall off the balcony, if that's what happened to her. Are you sure she didn't jump?"

"There's always that possibility. Did you know Kelly to speak to?"

"Sort of. We said hello now and again, and I helped her out when she had an electrical fault in the kitchen a few months back. Other than that, we didn't really have much time for each other. She seemed an okay kind of girl, no issues that I noticed. Worked hard. She got rid of that wastrel of a boyfriend, which was a bonus. He was always around here, trying to cadge something or other off me. Can't stand blokes like that."

"Did you know him?"

"Not personally. If you're asking me what his name was, it was Matt. But that's as much as I know."

"Who is it, Steve?" a woman's voice called from another room.

"It's the police, Sharon. I won't be a sec. Pause the movie for me... Sorry about that."

"There's no need. Any idea where this Matt hangs out? Where he works or lives perhaps?"

"What am I? The Oracle?" He grinned. "Sarcastic, I know. Sorry, no, I think he played snooker a lot, if that helps."

"Dare I ask where?"

"There's a hall in town, maybe ask down there. It's a shot in the dark, though."

"Okay, that's brilliant. Have you seen anyone around here acting suspicious in the last few days?"

He thought the question over for a while and then shrugged. "I don't think so, not off the top of my head. Want me to ask the missus for you?"

"If you wouldn't mind, thanks."

He pushed the door to a little and went back in the flat. He returned a while later. "Sorry, Sharon says she hasn't heard nor seen anything out of the ordinary lately, not that she can remember."

"Not to worry. Can I leave you one of my cards in case something comes to mind later?"

"Why not?" He took the card and shoved it in his pocket. "Anything else I can help with?"

"No, that's all. Thanks for speaking with me."

He gave a brief nod and closed the door. Sara walked past Carla who was talking to a young woman and knocked on the next door. There was no response. She took a step back and peered over the balcony opposite the flats. There was a car park directly below and a small play area with a few swings and a slide for the kids. Over to the left was a gang of youths, drinking from cans. Two of the youngsters had bikes, while the three others were either standing or perched on a small wall. *Could this be gang-related? Is it worth questioning them when we get downstairs?* No sooner had the thought crossed her mind than the boys threw their cans in the nearest bin and moved off.

"Penny for them?"

Sara slapped a hand over her chest and turned to face her partner. "Frighten the shit out of me, why don't you?"

"Sorry. I thought you heard me walk up behind you."

"I didn't. How did you get on?"

"The woman heard a scream earlier but thought nothing of it. It's normal for couples to have screaming matches around here, apparently."

"Bugger, that's not helpful, is it?" Sara peeked at her watch. "Jesus, it's half-seven already. Where does the bloody time go?"

"Yep, it's horrendous, and we've still got the mother to see yet. I don't know about you, but I'm dead on my feet."

"Me, too. Deep breath, let's hope our second wind kicks in soon. Let's go. We'll see the mother and then call it a day. I'll contact the station on the way, get them to organise the house-to-house enquiries, that'll save us a job. It's clear no one is going to admit to seeing anything, in my opinion."

"You think they're covering up? Maybe too scared to talk?"

"Who knows? Perhaps I'm reading more into the situation than is necessary."

They walked the length of the balcony and jumped into the lift.

Sara's nose twitched at the smell of urine flooding her nostrils. "I wish I'd taken an extra breath before embarking on the ride."

Carla chuckled and covered her nose with her hand. "I did."

"That's because you're smart, whereas I'm a knackered old bird."

"You do talk a load of shit at times."

The doors opened. Sara fished out her mobile and rang the station on the way to the cars. The officer on duty told her he'd arrange the house-to-house immediately.

"Okay, now that's done, we'll get over to see Patricia Pittman. I can't say I'm looking forward to it one iota. I hope she's sober when we get there."

"I doubt it, if what Audrey told us is true. I'll follow you out there."

Sara jumped behind the steering wheel and turned the radio up, hoping it would help keep her awake during the drive. The traffic was fair, not overly busy, so they made good time out to the woman's residence. The semi-detached property was in darkness. Sara had a sinking feeling as she got out of the car and joined Carla on the footpath outside the house.

"You think she's home?"

"Maybe she's passed out through the demon drink," Sara suggested. She groaned and pushed open the gate that led up a small path. Either side of the path the front garden had been decorated in slate chippings. There was the odd flowerpot dotted around, containing what appeared to be dead plants, unless they were dormant, ready to burst into bloom as the season progressed.

Sara rang the bell and waited. When there was no answer, she rang it a second time. The door was yanked open by a dishevelled woman with blonde hair whose roots needed touching up. She had a cigarette hanging out of her mouth, and her velour leisure suit had worn patches on the knees. *I dread to think how that happened.*

Sara flashed her ID in the woman's face. "Hello, Mrs Pittman. I'm DI Sara Ramsey, and this is my partner, DS Carla Jameson. Would it be all right if we came in for a moment to speak to you?"

"What for?" the woman slurred.

Jesus, her being paralytic is going to make our job a thousand trillion times worse. "It's of a personal nature. We'd rather not discuss it on the doorstep, if it's all the same to you."

She fell back against the hall wall and grunted, then she made a long sweeping gesture with her arm. Sara and Carla took a step into the house. That's when the reek of booze hit Sara. She coughed, not expecting to feel the waves of stale alcohol hit her with the force of a hundred-mile-an-hour gale.

Mrs Pittman slammed the door behind them. "Go on. Now you're in. Tell me why you're 'ere."

"Is it possible for us to go through to the lounge, perhaps?"

The woman launched herself off the wall and turned right into the lounge. Sara searched for the light switch at the doorway and flicked it on. The room was an utter mess. Plates with half-eaten food and used mugs filled the scratched black coffee table. Sticky patches marred the length and breadth of the table, in the areas where it wasn't cluttered. The rest of the furniture, even though it seemed fairly new, was riddled with food and drink stains, making Sara want to gag. Again, she cleared her throat before she motioned for the woman to take a seat.

"Oi, this is my house, not yours. I'll sit when I want to, not when some jumped-up frigging copper tells me to. Now get on with it, tell me why you're here and at this time of night. People have got lives to lead, you know. We've got a right to be at home, put our feet up and have a few bevvies when we want."

"I didn't say you couldn't. Please, we have some serious news to share with you, Mrs Pittman."

"It's Pat." She fell back into the chair and banged her head against the headrest. Rubbing it, she winced and stared at Sara. "Well, sit down then. I hate straining my neck looking up at you."

Sara and Carla both sat on the very edge of the sofa.

Inhaling a steadying breath, Sara began, "I'm sorry to put you out like this, but we have some bad news for you."

Pat crossed her arms, pouted and raised her eyebrows. "I'm listening."

"Earlier this evening, we were called to an incident in the city centre. When we got there, we found that a young woman had lost her life. We believe that woman is your daughter, Kelly."

Before Sara had revealed the name, Patricia let out a piercing scream, and her head lolled to one side. "No, no, no, not my baby as well."

Sara found herself glued to the spot. Ordinarily, she would have offered a comforting arm around the woman's shoulders and soothing words, but in this case, something held her back. *Is it because she's drunk and overreacting? Is she overreacting or is that just my perception of what's going on here? Or is it because of what Audrey told us about her not getting on well with Kelly lately?* Sara sensed Carla waiting for her to make a move. Eventually, she left her seat and crossed the room. She got down on one knee and tried to place an arm around Pat's shoulders, but the inebriated woman shrugged it off in anger and pushed Sara.

"Get away from me. How can she be dead?" Her words hadn't come out as slurred as when they'd first met her. There was a bottle of lager on the floor, the other side of her chair, and she swooped it up and downed the contents in one large gulp. Some of it dribbled out the side of her mouth, and she wiped the sleeve of her leisure top across her lips. There were no tears, not yet, in spite of the screaming and theatrics.

"Are you all right?" Sara dared to ask.

"What the fuck do you think? She was my only child, and I'll never see her again. I demand to know how she died."

Sara left the woman's side and returned to her seat beside Carla. "We believe she either fell from her balcony or was pushed. It's hard for us to determine at this early stage," Sara said cagily, ensuring she kept the truth from her for now, if only to gauge her reaction to the news. For all she knew, her mother might be the killer.

"What? She would never do it... take her own life like that. She had too much to live for."

"When was the last time you spoke to her?"

Pat's gaze scanned the room until she spotted something on a cluttered dining table against the far wall. She shot out of her chair, forgetting that she was two sheets to the wind, and toppled onto the floor. Again, Sara leapt up and offered the woman a hand. This time Pat accepted Sara's assistance and continued on her journey. Sara groaned inwardly once she realised what Pat was aiming for: yet another bottle of lager from a six-pack sitting on the edge of the table.

"Don't do it, Pat," she warned.

The woman turned sharply and bumped into the wall. "How dare you come into my home and start telling me what I can and can't do? You have no right. Get out!"

"We can't leave you like this. Is there anyone we can call to come and be with you? You shouldn't be left alone in this state."

"No. She was the only one I cared about." Pat dropped to the floor, buried her head in her hands and openly sobbed.

Sara looked over at Carla. "Can you put the kettle on?"

Carla rushed out of the room while Sara tried to get Pat up on her feet again.

Pat wrenched her arm out of Sara's hand and snapped at her, "Leave me alone. I told you to get out of here and I meant it. I need to grieve for my daughter."

"It would be better if you sat on the chair, Pat. We're only trying to help."

Pat got onto her hands and knees then clawed at the chair to help her get up onto her feet. Her body swayed violently in a circular motion. Then she heaved and threw up.

Sara's stomach groaned, and she swallowed down the bile burning her throat. She went in search of the kitchen and grumbled, "Shit, she's just puked in the living room."

"We should leave her to it. It's not our job to clear up after drunks, Sara."

"I know, but it's not in me to walk out and leave her like this. It's a sticky situation."

"Bugger, looks like we won't be getting home anytime soon."

"Sorry, Carla. You can shoot off, if that's what you want. I can't desert her."

"It's not our responsibility."

Sara sighed. "I'm all too aware of that." Her mobile rang, and her father's name filled the screen. She pressed the End Call button and vowed to ring him back after they left the house. For now, all her efforts and attention were needed to deal with the task at hand, getting Pat sobered up, if that was at all possible. "How's that cuppa coming along?"

"Leave it to me. You don't want one, do you?"

Sara peered into the coffee-stained mugs on the side and shook her head. "I'll pass. Thanks for the offer, though."

"Shall I make her a tea or coffee?"

"Take a punt on coffee. I'll go and see if she wants milk and sugar. My guess, looking at the state of those cups, is that she takes it black." She left the room and ventured back into the living room to find Pat trying her best to open another bottle of lager. Sara intervened and snatched the bottle from her hand.

Pat spun around and clouted Sara on the side of her face.

Shocked, Sara laid her hand on her cheek. "What was that for?"

"Stop interfering in my life. If I want a drink, I'll have one."

Sara pointed at the pile of vomit lying on the floor between them. "Don't you think you've had enough? Can you afford to waste drink like that? Knowing that as soon as it hits your stomach it's going to resurface?"

"Fuck off out of my house. Leave me alone." She plonked herself into one of the dining chairs at the table.

Sara left the room again, heaving at the smell emanating from the pile of sick soaking into the carpet, and returned to the kitchen.

"Does she?" Carla asked.

"What?"

"Take milk and sugar?"

Sara shook her head. "I wouldn't bother with either. I'm after a bucket, have you seen one?"

There was an alcove over to the left. Sara went in search of the cleaning equipment, hoping the woman actually possessed some, fearing the opposite was true. "Brilliant, I've found one."

Carla winced. "You're not going to clear it up, are you?"

"No way. I'm going to put the bucket over the top. She can clear up her own mess once we've gone. She wants us out of here. I need to see if she has any other relatives living in the area who can pop by and take over when we leave."

"Good luck with that one. Seeing the state she's in, I bet she's alienated most of her family over the last few months."

"I can't give up, not yet."

Carla poured the boiling water into the mug, and they both walked back into the living room. Pat's head was on her arm at the table.

Sara popped the bucket over the vomit and heaved, then she went

31

over to the table to check on the woman. "Pat, are you all right?"

She sat upright at the speed of lightning. "What do you think? I've just lost my daughter, that's on top of my husband dying a few months ago. I'll never be okay again."

"I'm sorry for your loss. Do you have any other members of your family living close by?"

"No. I wouldn't want the fuckers here anyway. Family sucks. The only time you ever see them is when they want something from you. Look around, I ain't got nothing, not now my husband and daughter are gone. I don't need anyone else. They all bled me dry years ago."

"What about friends? You must have a best friend you can count on?"

"Why must I? My daughter was my best friend, and now she's gone." The tears emerged once more.

"We can't leave you here like this, Pat. What about one of your neighbours?"

"What about them? All they do is complain every time I see them. I want nothing more to do with them. I'm fine. Leave me. I'm used to being on my own." She broke down again, this time sobbing her heart out.

Sara pulled out the chair next to her and pushed the cup of coffee in front of her. "We took a gamble and made you a black coffee, no sugar."

"Why are you being so nice to me?"

Sara smiled and covered the woman's hand with her own. "Believe it or not, because we care. Is that so hard to understand?"

"Yes. My daughter was the only one who cared, apart from my husband, but I drove her away."

"Why?"

"Because I thought she needed to get on with her life, not spend it moping around here with me. My husband was my soulmate. When he passed, I gave up, turned to drink as a way of coping with his loss. I regret driving her away now. Maybe if I hadn't, she would still be alive today. Do you think she killed herself? I could never forgive myself if that was the case."

Reluctantly, Sara shook her head. "No, I don't think that's likely. I wasn't going to tell you this but I think you should know. There were signs of a struggle in her flat."

Fresh tears coursed down Pat's cheeks. "Oh God. I can't believe anyone would want to hurt my baby. You know she was a nurse, don't you? She's been through a horrendous ordeal during the pandemic, caring for all those people who caught the disease, never to have recovered. Horrifying some of the stories she told me. She didn't deserve to lose her life." She gasped and asked, "You don't suppose this could have been because of her work, do you? What if a family member of a patient went after her, following the death of their loved one?"

Sara shrugged. "It's something to consider. The investigation has only just begun. Did she mention any problems of that ilk at all?"

Pat fished out a tissue from up her sleeve and wiped her cheeks and then her nose. "I haven't seen her in about six or seven weeks. I was too caught up in my own self-pitying world to get in touch with her. We had a blazing row back in January, and she stormed out of the house, told me she wouldn't come near me again until I sobered up. That's not likely to happen. Drink kills the emotions. Numbs the feelings of loss. Oh God, it's going to be worse still now. I might just end it all and be done with it. Do you think my husband and daughter will want to know me on the other side?"

Sara patted the back of her hand. "Don't think that way. We can get you the help you need. You don't have to go through this alone. There are grief counsellors available, especially to those desperate for help. Are you?"

"I don't know. If I sober up, how will I cope on my own?"

"You won't be alone. There are groups you can join, but you have to want to change in the first place. I can put you in touch with people, just say the word and I can make all the arrangements. You shouldn't have to cope with this situation alone, no one should."

"You'd go out of your way to help me? Why?"

"Because everyone deserves a chance in this life. Grief can destroy us, if we let it. Let me make a few calls now and get the ball rolling."

"I'm not sure I want a stranger nosing around in my life. Can I think it over?"

"Of course. No pressure from me. If you're sure you're going to be okay this evening, we'll leave you now. Here's my card. Give me a call when you've thought things over and tell me what you decide to do. There are always people willing to support you through your struggles."

Pat picked up the card and stared at it for a few seconds. She glanced up at Sara and nodded. "Thank you for caring."

"You're welcome. Now, is there anything else we can do for you before we leave?"

"I don't think so. I'm sorry you had to see me in this state. I loved my husband and my daughter so much…"

"It's clear to see. Ring me tomorrow."

She waved the card. "I will. Please, if Kelly was murdered, please find the person who did this to her."

"You have my word. Why don't you go to bed now? Have you eaten?"

"I had beans on toast earlier. It's enough. I don't eat much these days, the drink suppresses the hunger pangs."

"So I've heard. We'll drop back and see you in a few days, how's that?"

"I can't believe you're being so kind to me, I don't deserve it. Thank you."

Sara and Carla left the house.

Outside, Sara leaned against the bonnet of her car. "I had to show willing, the woman is in a right state."

"You're too kind-hearted at times. I would have walked out and not even left her my card."

Sara shook her head. "You might say that, but if it came to the crunch, you wouldn't have ditched her. You haven't got it in you to be so mean."

"Glad you have faith in me. What now?"

"Now, we go home and start afresh in the morning."

"Okay, I won't argue. It's getting late."

Sara looked at her watch. It was almost ten o'clock. Where had the evening gone? "Damn, my father rang, I should call him back, but they usually go to bed early. I'll feel their wrath if I wake them up. I'll give him a call in the morning. Go, Carla, thanks for tagging along with me this evening. I hope you manage to get some rest when you get home."

"I'll grab something from the takeaway on the way and then flop into bed."

"Send my apologies to Des for keeping you so late this evening."

"I won't. It's my life. I'm tougher than I used to be where men are concerned. Either he accepts my coming home late or he doesn't. I'm not one for pandering to blokes any longer."

Sara punched the air. "Yes, spoken like a true independent woman."

Carla sniggered. "I know, right? It's about time."

They both laughed and went their separate ways. Sara drove home, her mind whirling with different scenarios as to what might have happened to Kelly Pittman. Unable to switch off, she pulled up outside her small detached house on the new estate, to find Mark on the doorstep, cradling Misty in his arms.

He leaned forward to kiss her. She returned the kiss and at the same time stroked Misty's head.

Mark handed Misty over for a cuddle. "She's been meowing for you."

Unexpected tears emerged. She kissed Misty's head over and over until her purring became loud and rattling. "You are so precious to me, both of you. Never forget that."

Mark frowned and guided them through the front door. "What's all this? We know how much we mean to you. I'm guessing you've had an emotionally tough day, am I right?"

Sara popped Misty on the floor and removed her coat. Mark took it from her and hung it on the rack. She slipped off her shoes and neatly placed them next to his then wrapped her arms around his neck. "You could say that. Another young woman's life ended through what appears to be a vicious crime. It saddens me to think this is the norm these days. When did a life stop being valuable? How can some people easily take the life of another and go on as if nothing has happened?

I'm not saying that's the case with this investigation, but jeez, when is all this violence towards others going to end? Has this pandemic not taught us anything?"

He gathered her in his arms and ran a soothing hand down her back. "You're tired and emotional. Have you eaten tonight?"

"You're right. I am. No, Carla and I went straight to the crime scene. I'm not sure I could stomach any food."

"Give it a try. I made your favourite, a lasagne."

"What? You're too good to me."

He pushed her away from him and kissed her. "Nonsense, what else was I going to do with my evening without you to keep me company?"

They parted, and it was then that the delicious aroma hit her. "Why hadn't I smelt that before?"

He smiled and walked into the kitchen. "Go in the lounge, the fire is on, put your feet up. I won't be long."

"You spoil me," she called after him.

"I know, it's the reason I swooped into your life."

Misty followed her into the lounge. Sara flicked through the stations until she found the local news. There was a reporter at this evening's crime scene, filling the public in on what they'd managed to find out from the residents about the case. Sara hoped Pat wasn't watching.

Mark appeared with a large portion of lasagne and a slice of garlic bread. "Blimey, I'll never eat all this."

"You will."

He knew she would, experience told them both that she wouldn't be able to leave any. Fifteen minutes later, she mopped up the juice with a second piece of garlic bread he'd fetched from the kitchen. She leaned back and let out a satisfied groan. "I reckon that must be your best lasagne yet. I wish I could cook like you. My attempts are dire in comparison to what you conjure up."

"You'll never starve when I'm around, love."

She kissed him and rested her head on his chest. He removed the plate from her lap and pulled her in closer. Sara drifted off to sleep moments later, exhausted from her fifteen-hour shift.

2

*S*ara woke the next morning and glanced around at the familiar surroundings of their bedroom. Mark stirred beside her. "How did I get up here?"

"I must admit to regretting giving you such a huge portion for dinner last night after carrying you up the stairs. Nearly broke my back."

She sniggered and snuggled up to him. "You should have woken me. What time did we come to bed?"

"Around midnight. Umm… your father has rung a few times during the night."

She sat upright and grabbed her mobile off the bedside table. "What? Oh God, that's unusual for him. He rang while I was breaking the sad news to the victim's mother last night and I forgot to call him back—actually, it was too late to ring him, I'd better do it now." She returned her father's call, dread seeping through her. "Dad, I'm so sorry. I had the day from hell yesterday and I forgot to return your call. What's wrong? Are you all right?"

"That's okay, dear, I realise how busy you are. I'm okay. I'm sitting here at the hospital."

"What? Why? Oh no, is something wrong with Mum?"

There was a short silence followed by a long sigh from her father. "You'd better get here, Sara. I'll fill you in when you arrive."

Sara threw back the quilt and tore around the room collecting fresh underwear from the drawer and a clean suit from the wardrobe. "What's wrong, Dad?"

"When you get here, dear. Promise me you'll drive safely."

"I will. Where are you? In A and E?"

"No, we're on the Women's Ward."

"Okay, I think I know where that is. I'll be there as soon as I can. I love you, Dad."

"We love you, too, sweetheart. Drive carefully."

She chose to have a quick wash rather than a shower and was dressed, ready to leave ten minutes later.

"Calm down, Sara. You're going to be no good to anyone if you tear around and drive like a maniac."

"I know." She stood and gulped down several deep breaths to calm her thundering heart. "But hospital? What the dickens is she doing there? Something drastic must have happened. I know what Mum's like, she wouldn't go near the place if it wasn't necessary."

"There's no point in you speculating. Do you want me to call work for you?"

"No, I'll ring Carla on the way."

"If you're sure. Will you let me know what's going on later? As soon as you know anything. I'll be worried about her until I hear from you."

"Of course, it goes without saying. I'd better fly. I love you." Sara crushed him to her for the briefest of moments and then raced down the stairs. At the bottom she called up, "Can you feed Misty for me?"

"Consider it done. Go. Drive safely."

"I will. Speak later," she shouted back, grappling with her coat and slipping her shoes on at the same time, struggling not to topple over in her haste.

The traffic was atrocious the closer she got to town. Aware that it was against the regulations, she hit the siren and swerved her way through the town and drew up outside the hospital a few minutes later.

Fortunately, she found a free space in the car park closest to the main entrance.

Carla had been shocked when she'd rung her en route and instructed Sara to contact her as soon as she had any news.

Sara wound her way through the reception area and asked the young brunette behind the desk where the Women's Ward was, after her mind suddenly went blank.

Directions obtained, she hopped in the lift and made her way up to the third floor. The closer she got to the ward the faster her heart pounded. *Damn, what am I going to find when I get there? Don't think about it. Maybe Mum had a fall and bumped her head.* Dozens of possible scenarios swam through her mind. Arriving at the ward, she slathered the antiseptic gel on her hands and pushed through the door, freezing on the spot while she scanned the ward in search of her father.

"Can I help?" a nurse called over from behind the desk.

"I'm looking for my mother. Sorry, Elizabeth Beaumont."

"Ah, yes. I'll show you the way. Your father is sitting with her."

"Is she all right? What's wrong with her?"

The nurse smiled and motioned for Sara to follow her across the ward to where the curtains were drawn around the final bed. "She's in there. Be gentle with them."

Sara frowned, puzzled by what the nurse could mean. She pulled back the curtain to find her mother lying in bed with her eyes closed, ashen in colour, and her father sitting beside her, his head resting on his arms on the bed. "Dad," she whispered, not wishing to wake her mother. Receiving no response, she took a step closer and patted her father gently on the back. "Dad. I'm here."

He stirred, sat up and stretched.

Sara flew into his arms. "Dad, what's going on? Why is Mum here? She looks dreadful."

"We should get a coffee. I could do with a bacon sandwich. I've been here all night with her."

"Of course."

They made their way to the hospital canteen. Her father didn't say a word on the way which only caused Sara to be even more concerned.

Finally, once they had their sandwiches and coffee in front of them, he told her what was going on.

"Your mother took a turn for the worse last night. I felt it best if she came to the hospital. She tried to object, but I put my foot down for a change. You know as well as I do how stubborn she can be."

"I know. What sort of turn, Dad?"

He stared at his sandwich and finally took a bite. Sara did the same with her breakfast. Once he'd finished his mouthful, her father confided, "Your mother has been ill for months. She threatened to divorce me if I told you."

Sara flung herself back in her chair. "What? How ill? What's wrong with her?"

He took a sip from his coffee and, avoiding any form of eye contact, continued, "Your mother was diagnosed with liver cancer a few months ago."

Sara was stunned by the news. Her anger mounted as soon as the shock dissipated. Sitting forward, she demanded, "Why? Why keep this from me?"

He sucked in a shuddering breath. "It was her decision, Sara. She's seen you so happy these last couple of years since Mark came into your life, she didn't want to ruin it by telling you how sick she was."

She shook her head in disbelief. "How sick is she?" Her hands clenched into fists.

"It's pretty bad, love. She's had a few rounds of chemo but…"

"But? Dad, you need to tell me everything now. What's the prognosis?"

Her father pushed his plate away and swiped at the stray tear which had dripped onto his cheek. "It's terminal."

Those two words made Sara's world grind to a halt. She stared at her father for a long time before she finally found the courage to ask, "How long has she got?"

"Weeks, maybe days. They've got her dosed up on morphine to suppress the pain. I don't know how I'm going to cope without her, Sara."

She left her chair, rushed around the table and knelt beside him.

"You'll cope, Dad. We both will. I wish you'd told me. I could have been prepared for this day. Maybe the doctor is wrong. Have you thought about getting a second opinion? Have you seen the oncologist?"

"Yes, we've been under the oncologist for months. He's the one who gave us the grave news. I don't want to lose her. She's my world, Sara. I wouldn't be able to cope with life if she isn't around."

She hugged her father and sobbed. "We'll get through this together, Dad. She knows how much we love her. I just wish you'd both told me. To find out this way is so…"

He pulled away and cradled her face between his withering hands. "It was her decision, not mine. I would have told you in a heartbeat, sweetheart. Please, please, forgive me."

She removed his hands from her face and kissed each of them. "Nothing to forgive. I know you had your reasons to keep quiet. Will Mum be able to come back home?"

"I'm hoping so. The pain was excruciating for her to cope with, I felt it best for her to be here, where they could keep a close eye on her. I don't mind telling you, love, I'm petrified of what lies ahead of us."

"What about Lesley, does she know?"

"No. We've kept it from your sister as well. I tried to call her last night, but she was out with her friends. I left a message on her phone to ring me, but I've heard nothing since."

"She's got the day off today, she's probably still tucked up in bed nursing a hangover. I'll try and get in touch with her after we've eaten." She returned to her seat and pushed the plate back in front of her father. "Eat it, Dad, you need to keep your strength up."

Her father smiled and took a bite out of his sandwich. Sara sipped her drink and studied her father, for the first time seeing his true age. He was sixty-six now, and her mother was sixty-five. Her father's own health had to be monitored regularly by the doctor. She feared if anything happened to her mother, which was inevitable, given what her father had just told her, he would go downhill quickly himself.

Her father's mobile rang. "It's Lesley. Will you speak to her?"

Sara held out her hand to accept the phone. "Lesley, it's me."

"Sara. Shit, is everything all right? I've just woken up to find a message from Dad asking me to ring him."

"Are you sitting down?"

"Yes, I'm still in bed. Now you're scaring me, just tell me, Sara."

"We're at the hospital. Mum took a turn last night and was rushed in. I think you should come, hon."

"What? Oh shit. Why did I have to go out last night? I had a skinful. I'll call a taxi and be with you soon. What ward?"

"Women's Ward, third floor. Take your time, there's no need to rush."

"Okay. Give Mum and Dad a hug from me."

"I will. See you soon." Sara ended the call and placed her father's phone back on the table.

"She's going to be livid when I reveal the truth."

"You're right, but she'll soon calm down. Neither of us should have discovered the truth this way, Dad. We had a right to know long before it got to this stage."

"I couldn't argue with your mother's wishes, I refused to do that, love."

"I understand your reasons, at least, I think I do. It's such a mess. We could have helped out with Mum's care if we'd known the facts."

"You're both busy people. You have your own lives to lead, Sara. Please, don't make me feel any worse than I already do."

"All right. Lecture over. We need to look to the future now. What has the doctor told you?"

"They're going to monitor her for the next few days. Administer the pain relief and see how she responds to that before they make any further assessments of her needs."

"Is there any chance the cancer will disappear?"

"No, love. There's no going back once we reach the terminal stage."

Sara's chest constricted as if an invisible hand was squeezing her heart. She reached out to her father. He gathered her hand in both of his and looked her in the eye. "I'm sorry, Dad. For all of us."

"We need to remain strong in your mother's presence. I have grave fears about Lesley on that score. You know how much she loves to fly off the handle."

"I'll have a word with her when she arrives. Warn her to tone it down a bit."

"Thanks, love. We'd better be getting back in case your mother wakes up and panics that I'm not there beside her."

They left the canteen and returned to the ward to find Sara's mother awake. She seemed shocked and taken aback to see Sara standing next to her father. Her voice cracked a little when she accused her father of telling her. "I thought we said we were going to keep this between us."

"I had to tell her, love. Don't be mad at me." Her father retook his seat beside her mother, and Sara bent to kiss her mum.

"Don't have a go at him, Mum. He did the right thing. Lesley is on her way."

Her mother squeezed her eyes shut and rested her head back against the pillow. "Oh no. I'll never hear the end of it now."

"She'll be fine. I'll take her to one side and have a word with her when she gets here."

"My life is going to be hell for a few days," her mother complained further.

"It won't. No one wants to cause you more stress than is necessary, Mum. You should have told us. We had a right to know."

Her mother teared up. "I was doing my best to protect you both. Your father and I coped with the news between us."

"Dad told me the thought process behind your decision; it still wasn't right to keep us out of the loop. Is there anything you need right now?"

"Only to rest. I'm in constant pain and haven't been sleeping well lately. I collapsed last night and by the time I came round your father had rung for an ambulance."

"He did the right thing. You're in the best place now."

"Mum! Oh God, look at you."

Sara almost jumped out of her skin. Lesley had snuck up behind her. Lesley barged past to get to her mother.

"Now don't you go overreacting, Lesley. I'm fine. Go with your sister, she'll tell you what's going on. Don't make a fuss on the ward, I don't want you to disturb the other patients."

Sara tugged on her sister's arm, and together they left the ward. Outside, Sara ordered her sister to take a seat and sat beside her. "I need to tell you that Mum and Dad have been keeping something from us for months."

"What? Tell me."

Sara latched on to her sister's hand and held it firmly. "Mum's got cancer."

Lesley gasped and yanked her hand from Sara's. "No way. She would have told us."

Sara shook her head. "It was Mum's decision not to, so don't go blaming Dad."

"Are you sure they didn't tell you?"

"I swear to you, I only found out less than an hour ago, around the time you bothered to ring Dad back."

"Bothered? I was out of it! Don't put the blame on me just because I've got a life."

Sara tilted her head back and studied the ceiling. "I wasn't. Can we put a halt to the bitchiness now and put our heads together for a change?"

"About what? Do you want to put 'our heads together' to say some kind of spell to make all this go away, is that it?"

"Cut the sarcasm, Lesley. I appreciate you're still hungover from last night, but don't take it out on me. I put in a fifteen-hour day yesterday and then woke up this morning, exhausted, and got summoned here. So no, my day isn't faring too well right now either."

Lesley rolled her eyes and chewed on her thumbnail. "I'm sorry," she mumbled.

"The last thing Mum and Dad want is for us to fall out with each other. They're going to need us both to remain strong, to help guide them through this godawful situation, at least Dad will."

"I know you're going to think I'm selfish when I say this, but I'm not strong enough to do it, Sara."

"You are. You have to be. We have to be stronger than we've ever

44

been in our lives before. We've both been dealt raw deals in the past, some greater than others, but we got through the trials and tribulations as a family. We can do this, together, as a family."

"How long has she got?" Lesley ran a hand through her tangled hair. Her fingers tugged at a knot. "Ouch!"

Sara sank a hand into her handbag and withdrew a comb. "Here, sort yourself out. Maybe weeks, that's all. Dad said they're waiting for the doctor to come and see Mum to give them a proper prognosis. Either way, she hasn't got long. Hence the necessity for us to work together and not be at each other's throat right now."

Her sister pulled the comb through her long hair and winced several times as it hit a few more knots. She handed it back to Sara. "I don't want to be at loggerheads with you. Mum should come first, I'm in agreement with that." Suddenly, Lesley broke down.

A significant lump formed in Sara's throat, and she slung an arm around her sister and pulled her close. "Don't do this. Not now. We have to go back in there soon, it would tear them apart if they saw your red eyes and tear-stained cheeks."

"I can't help it. In a few weeks she could be gone. How am I supposed to feel about that?"

"It's something we're going to have to get used to, love. No matter how difficult it may be."

"Why are you being so practical about this, don't you care?"

Sara shot back in her chair and stared at her sister. "What? You think this is bloody easy for me? I'm devastated by the news, how dare you think otherwise? What's the point in us crumbling, though?"

"All right, I'm sorry. I didn't mean anything by that. You've always been the more practical one." Lesley covered her face with her hands and wept.

Sara struggled to hold it together, watching her sister fall apart in front of her eyes. "Lesley, please, stay strong. We're going to have to go back in there in a moment. Mum and Dad will be watching out for telltale signs, to see how we're coping with the news. Don't let them see that you've been crying, please."

After wiping her eyes on the sleeve of her jacket, Lesley sniffed and stared at her. "It's so hard. The truth is, I'm not coping, they're going to see that, eventually."

Sara hugged her. What else could she say that she hadn't spent the last ten minutes saying? How could she offer her sister advice on how to handle the shocking news when she hadn't really had time to wrap her head around things herself?

She glanced the length of the hallway and spotted a sign for the toilets halfway down on the right. "Let's freshen up in the loos before we go back in there."

Five minutes later, the two sisters returned to the ward to stand alongside their parents. Sara could tell her parents were both upset. Her mother's eyes were red from crying. She bent down and kissed her on the cheek. "We love you, Mum."

Her mother broke down again, and her father comforted her. "There, there, everything is going to be all right," her father whispered.

Except, it wasn't. Life would never be the same again once her mother passed away. Sara pushed the depressing thought aside to deal with the here and now. The curtain drew back a little, and a doctor appeared.

"Would you mind leaving us alone for a moment?" he asked, his question aimed at Sara and Lesley.

"No, I want them to hear what you have to say, Doctor. They're my family, I've kept enough from them. I have no intention of keeping anything else from them."

The doctor nodded his understanding and shuffled his feet. "Very well. I'm sorry, the news isn't good. Things have progressed faster than we anticipated. The scan has revealed that the cancer has spread to your lungs."

Her mother swallowed hard. "How long have I got?"

"Days rather than weeks. I'm so sorry to be the bearer of such grave news. We're going to do our very best to make you feel more comfortable. My advice would be for you to remain in hospital... until the end."

"Thank you for being honest with me, Doctor. I'm sure you have other patients you need to see." Her mother smiled weakly and dismissed him.

The doctor seemed awkward; he gave a brief nod and left them. Sara felt like someone had punched her several times in the gut. Her legs weakened, but she gave herself a good talking-to. *You have to remain strong, if only for Dad's and Lesley's sakes.*

"Now don't you dare go getting upset, girls. My time has come. We're all going to need to deal with that. The last thing I want is for my final days on this earth to be maudlin, that's not us at all, is it?"

Lesley's shoulders shook as the tears cascaded. "Oh, Mum. I wish you'd told us. We would have been more prepared..."

Her mother reached for Lesley's hand. "Come, child. I didn't want to burden you. Your father and I made the decision together. I'm tired now. I'd like you all to leave so I can get some rest."

"In other words, you want us to get on with our lives," Sara added. She took a step forward and kissed her mother. "I love you, Mum. We'll be here for when you need us."

"I love you, too, my precious daughters. Now go. You have work to go to, Sara, don't let this disrupt your life."

"Work can wait."

"I insist. You go now. I appreciate you coming, but it's time for you and Lesley to leave. I want to be alone with your father. We have a lot to discuss."

"But, Mum..." Lesley began until Sara tugged on her arm.

"Come on, sis. Let's leave them to it."

Sara hugged her mother and father and waited for her sister to do the same, then they left the ward, arm in arm.

"Do you need me to give you a lift home?" Sara asked once they'd reached the main entrance.

"No. I think I'll go for a walk down by the river to clear my head."

"Are you sure you're all right? I can hang around and have a coffee, if you need to chat."

"No. I'll be fine. I need time alone, to put things back into perspective."

"Sounds like a good idea. Give me a ring if you need to chat, okay?"

Lesley sniffled. "I will. It's going to take a while to get my head around things, but I'll do it. I have to. Poor Dad, how's he going to cope without her? She does everything around the house, takes care of all the bills, the financial side of things, the cleaning, the cooking."

"We'll have to help out there for a while. He's going to be lost for the first few months." Sara sighed. "Aren't we all? But we'll get there. Okay, I'm going to shoot off now. Stay strong and don't hesitate to give me a call if you need to chat. I know you, you bottle things up. That's the worst thing you can do right now, hon."

"I hear you. Thanks, sis. I don't know how you manage to stay so positive."

She was crumbling inside but she had no intention of telling her sister that. "We do what we have to do, sis."

They shared a final hug, and then the sisters parted.

Sara drove to the station on autopilot, her thoughts with her parents, wishing that she could have stayed longer at the hospital with them.

The desk sergeant, Jeff, greeted her with a warm smile. "Not a bad morning, ma'am."

"Weather-wise, no, Jeff. Have a good day."

He frowned. "Everything all right?"

"It will be, eventually. Must dash, I'm behind as it is."

Sara entered the incident room under the gaze of her team. "Sorry I'm late. I might as well tell you all what's going on. My mother was rushed into hospital last night. She and my father thought it best not to tell me and my sister that Mum has cancer. Unfortunately, she's classed as terminal and it has now turned into a waiting game."

"Shit! I'm so sorry, Sara," Carla whispered to the side of her, forgetting the rule about calling her *boss* in front of the rest of the team. "Is there anything we can do to help?"

"No, nothing. I need to throw myself into work, get my mind off what's going on. So, if someone wants to shout me a cup of coffee, we'll run through where we stand with the investigation."

Craig jumped to his feet. "I'll get it. Anyone else want one?"

"Me, please," Carla shouted, followed by the rest of the team.

Craig was kept busy for the next five minutes, ferrying the cups around the room.

Sara sipped at her coffee and glanced up at the clock; it was already ten-thirty. Once Craig was seated again, Sara addressed the team. "Okay, as you're probably aware by now, Carla and I had a busy evening yesterday. The crime scene was horrendous. Our initial assessment is that someone probably pushed Kelly Pittman over the balcony of her flat. Her neighbour found her and rang nine-nine-nine. Kelly was a nurse in the Accident and Emergency Department at Hereford Hospital. We visited her mother last night. Although she was three sheets to the wind, we managed to obtain some information from her. Namely that Kelly had recently split up with a boyfriend. However, it was a neighbour who told us that the boyfriend liked snooker. So that's where we'll begin digging. I don't know what the answer is, but there can't be too many snooker halls in Hereford, can there?"

"I can think of one off the top of my head," Barry was the first to say. "I used to go there regularly. I haven't been for a while, though. I can search, see if that's still the only one in the area, if you like?"

"Yes, do that. I don't suppose you know a Matt from your time visiting the venue, do you?"

He shrugged. "Not really one for mixing with strangers, boss. I go there for the snooker, sod everything else. Gemma only allows me a couple of hours off at a time."

They all laughed.

"What?" he shouted, somewhat offended. "I do my best helping out with the baby most nights when I get home."

She smiled. "That's admirable of you, Barry. Don't mind us, we're just joshing with you. Okay, the only other avenue we can go down is to visit her place of work, see if she's had any hassle in the department lately. We all know how shitty people can get if they're left hanging around for hours. Maybe she had a current boyfriend, perhaps a work colleague can fill us in where her mother couldn't."

49

"Do you want me to go to the hospital?" Craig raised a hand and asked.

"We'll see. I think it's something Carla and I should tackle. We're waiting for the forensic results from her flat. We found numerous patches of blood, so we believe a kerfuffle of sorts took place, obviously before her death. One neighbour was out, and another neighbour heard her scream, presumably during her fall. We left uniform conducting the house-to-house enquiries—that's another angle we need to chase up this morning. Craig, why don't you do that for me?"

He nodded and took a sip from his coffee.

Sara did the same and then continued. "The victim's bag was left at the scene. Her purse was still inside, so I think we can rule out burglary. In my opinion, I believe this was more likely to have been a personal attack and therefore we're dealing with a murder inquiry as opposed to a possible suicide. After we spoke to the victim's mother, we discovered Kelly's father also died a few months ago. Can you recall how he died, Carla?"

"No, I can't. Want me to look into it?"

"Yes, let's cover all the angles from the word go. If he died in suspicious circumstances then it's likely the two deaths might be linked. And that's about it. Christine, I'd like you and Jill to go through the financial side of things, to see if there's anything suspicious there. Apart from that, we've got very little to go on for now. Right, I'll be in my office dealing with the dreaded post, not that I'm in the right frame of mind to deal with that. Give me half an hour, Carla, and then we'll visit her place of work."

Carla gave her the thumbs-up. Sara picked up her cup and left the team to it. She ventured into her office and gave her desk a cursory glance then perched on the edge of it to take in the glorious views of the Brecon Beacons that always seemed to balance her stressful daily life. Her mobile rang, and she looked at the name on the screen. "Damn, I forgot to ring Mark." She sat in her chair and answered the call. "Hi, Mark, sorry, I hadn't forgotten, honestly. I've only just got into work."

"There's no need for you to apologise. How did it go at the hospital? Is everything all right?"

"I was hoping to tell you the news in person, but I don't think it should wait."

"Oh heck, that sounds worrying."

Sara inhaled a steadying breath and fought hard to keep the emotion out of her voice. "Mum's got cancer. She's had it for months and she and Dad decided between them to keep it from me and Lesley."

"What? Damn. How serious is it, Sara?"

"Very. The doctor told us it's terminal. It started out as liver cancer and now it has spread to her lungs."

Silence filled the line, and then Mark cleared his throat and asked, "How long has she got?"

"Days rather than weeks."

"Jesus, I'm so sorry. How are you holding up? Should you be at work?"

"What else would I do? Sit at home, mulling things over? I can't do that. I'd rather be here, keeping my mind active. I'm distraught, we all are."

"I can imagine. Your father is going to need us all to remain upbeat."

"I know. I issued Lesley the same lecture not half an hour ago at the hospital."

"It wasn't supposed to come across as a lecture."

"Sorry, I know. My emotions are all over the place. I'm trying desperately not to think of what it means to us as a family right now."

"I understand completely. I'm at the end of the phone if you need to speak to me, love."

"I know you are, sweetheart. I'm going to crack on with my working day now. We'll have a chat about the situation this evening. Why don't we go to the pub for a meal, for a change?"

"Suits me. I'll book a table. For around seven, yes?"

"Sounds perfect. I love you, Mark."

"Right backatcha. And Sara…"

"Yes?"

"Don't push me away. We deal with what lies ahead of us as a team, all right?"

"I know. I have no intention of pushing you away, I assure you. See you tonight." She ended the call and let out a large breath.

Carla appeared in the doorway. "How are you coping?"

"I've just broken the news to Mark. I'll admit, but only to you, that I'm an emotional wreck. I'm going to need your help to get me through the day, Carla."

"I'm always here for you. Would you rather I carried out the interviews at the hospital with someone else?"

"No, I'll tag along, but yes, if you'll take the lead to ease the burden on me."

"You only have to ask. You can whip my arse if I screw up."

Sara smiled at her partner. "You won't. I have every confidence in you. Thanks, Carla. How's Des?"

"He's fine. We stayed up past midnight last night and sorted through another half a dozen boxes. It's surprising how much crap we gather over the years, isn't it?"

"I remember thinking the same when I moved into my place. I'm glad to see you so happy. He's a good man."

"I have you to thank for getting us together." She held up her crossed fingers. "So far, I know I've done the right thing moving in with him. Who's to say if things will change further down the line?"

"Ever the pessimist. Only if you allow things to. Just be aware that a relationship needs two people to work at it, not just one. There are always compromises to be made on both sides. You two were made for each other, take my word for it."

"Thanks. I hope so. Anyway, we're engaged now, so we've got to make a go of things."

"I'd forgotten all about that. Too right. Have you set a date yet?"

"No, we haven't had time to sit down and discuss it, what with him moving from Worcester and all that entailed. Plus, him trying to fit into his new role around here."

"It's been a whirlwind couple of months for sure. Your feet haven't touched the ground in that time, I bet."

"Too right. Okay, I think you've had enough distractions for one day, I'll leave you to deal with the post."

"Did you manage to chase up forensics?"

"I did. They're snowed under and promised to get back to us when they can."

"Same old news there then. Okay, I'll take a quick look through this lot and be with you in a little while."

There was a knock on the door. Sara frowned and shouted, "Come in."

The last person she expected to poke her head into the room was the DCI. "Can I come in?"

Sara motioned at the chair in front of her and dismissed Carla. "I won't be long."

Carla left them to it.

"This is unexpected, boss. What can I do for you?"

Carol Price settled into her chair, a serious expression set in stone. "I dropped in earlier, but Carla told me you were at the hospital, something about your mother?"

"Sorry, I should have come by to fill you in." She swallowed down the lump that had forced its way into her throat.

"Is everything all right, Sara?"

The emotion whooshed through her like a tsunami. "No, not really." Her voice faltered, and she cleared her throat. "Mum has terminal cancer. I might need some time off soon, possibly to care for her, I don't think my father will be able to cope alone. No, wait, the doctor advised us that she should stay in hospital until the end." The words rushed out of her. She sucked in a breath once she'd revealed the extent of her mother's plight.

Carol ran a hand around her face. "Oh my. I truly wasn't expecting you to say that. You and your family must be devastated. How long has she got?"

"The doctor reckons days, maybe weeks, no longer than that. It's hard to get my head around, if I'm honest with you."

"Don't even try. Sara, I can't believe you're here. Take some time off, you're going to need to see more of your mother before…"

"Before it's too late, you mean? I'll be there if they need me. In the meantime, I think it would be preferable to stay at work. It'll help keep my mind off things, but I appreciate the offer."

"I'm so sorry you and your family are going through this. You know you've only got to ask for time off and you can have it, right?"

"I know. Thanks all the same. A new case landed on my desk last night. I'm prepared to give it my all as usual. We'll see how things go later on as to whether I take you up on your kind offer."

"Let's get one thing straight, it's not me being kind, you're entitled to the time off, if you think you might need it. You work far too hard as it is, it's the least we can do."

Sara's cheeks glowed. "Carla and I are just on our way out, back to the hospital, in fact."

Carol frowned. "May I ask why?"

"I should have said. The latest victim was a nurse."

"Bugger. What happened?"

"We believe she was pushed over her balcony. She lived in one of the high-rise blocks of flats in town. There were blood patches inside her flat, so it would appear she put up a bit of a fight before the murderer dropped her from a great height."

"Shit! I was going to ask if we could be dealing with a suicide. I guess we can rule that out when the evidence is pointing to the contrary."

"Yep, that was our initial thought, too. We soon changed our minds."

"Well, I'll leave you to it then. You know where I am, if you should need a chat, either professionally or personally. Take care, Sara. Don't put yourself under too much stress."

"I won't. I've already told Carla that she's going to take the lead during the interviews today."

"Good for you. You can stand back and jump in if she misses anything important."

"I'm hoping that won't be the case. We'll see."

Sara followed the chief out of the office.

3

*S*ara had the jitters being back at the hospital; she was tempted to pay her mother another visit. Instead, she ignored the urge and got on with the business at hand.

Carla must have sensed the change in her demeanour because she nudged her arm as they entered the main entrance and asked, "Are you sure you're up to this?"

"Yes, with you taking the lead. Don't worry about me."

"Okay. I don't mind telling you that I'm a touch nervous. It's like doing an exam while the headmistress is standing over you, waiting for you to screw up."

Laughing, Sara patted her on the back. "You'll be fine. I have complete faith in you. Just don't forget to introduce yourself properly to everyone you interview."

"I won't. Thanks for the timely reminder." With that, Carla withdrew her warrant card and approached the receptionist. "Sorry to trouble you. I'm DS Jameson, and this is DI Ramsey. We're hoping to have a chat with the person who is in charge of the Accident and Emergency Department. Would they be available, please?"

The receptionist's brow furrowed. "I'll have to check. I won't be a moment." She left her seat and dipped into an office a few feet behind her. She emerged a little while later with an older woman whose smile was playing hide and seek.

"Can I help?" she asked abruptly.

"Only if you're the person in charge of A and E. Are you?" Carla replied, holding her nerve.

"I'm not. As you can imagine, they're seriously busy down there at all hours of the day. The last thing they need is to be bothered with police enquiries. So, I'm going to repeat myself, can I help?"

Sara bit down on her tongue and allowed Carla to handle the officious-sounding woman.

"And I'll repeat, not unless you're the person I'm looking for. Now, if you'd be kind enough to tell me where to find them."

"May I ask what this is about?"

"Does it matter?" Carla responded, her tone matching the woman's.

"I can see we're getting nowhere fast here. Doctor Saunders is the person you're after, he's a very busy man. I'll see if he can spare you a few minutes."

"Thank you. That's all we were after." Carla turned her back on the woman and rolled her eyes at Sara. "Thought I'd screwed up there for a second."

"You did exceptionally well. You know we often come up against objectionable people now and again. Bravo."

"Thanks. Good job she couldn't see my hands, I was shaking like a leaf."

The woman appeared in front of them again and pointed down the hallway. "Go to the end and turn right. Doctor Saunders has told me he can spare you five minutes now, if you hurry."

"Thanks for your assistance," Carla replied.

They tore down the corridor and saw a man in a blue uniform pacing the area at the bottom. Sara and Carla extracted their IDs. Again, Sara left Carla to take up the reins.

"Thank you for seeing us, Doctor Saunders. I'm DS Jameson, and this is my partner, DI Ramsey."

"The receptionist said this was urgent. Do you mind telling me why you want to see me?"

"As you're the person in charge, we'd like to ask you a few questions about one of the nurses who works here."

"Which one?"

"Kelly Pittman. Do you know her?"

"Of course I do. Why?"

"Unfortunately, she lost her life yesterday."

His head jutted forward, and he raked a trembling hand through his hair. "What? Are you sure? She was here, on shift yesterday."

"We're sure. We've positively identified the victim."

He tutted and shook his head. "I need to sit down. Come into my office."

They followed him through a door and into an office off to the left.

Sara noted the colour had drained from his lightly tanned face as he took his seat. "Are you all right, Doctor?" she asked.

"Not really. As well as being part of our team... Kelly and I had just started seeing each other. Not that it's common knowledge because it's frowned upon for staff to fraternise at work. She was in the process of switching roles, awaiting an opportunity to arise. Shit! How did she die? Was it an accident?"

Sara mentally took a step back again.

Carla pushed on. "We believe we're dealing with a murder inquiry, sir."

"Please, sit down. I can't believe what I'm hearing. Who? Why? Oh God, it wasn't her ex, was it?"

"We're at the initial stages of our investigation. Do you happen to know much about her ex?"

"I know he's a tosser. He showed up here a few times, drunk, asking for money. I had to take her to one side, to reprimand her. That's when she broke down and revealed that he abused her and she was desperate to get him out of her life."

"And what was your response to hearing that news?" Carla asked. She turned to Sara and handed over her notebook. "Can you take down some notes for me? Thank you."

Sara suppressed a giggle. "Of course I can."

"What was the outcome, do you know?" Carla asked.

"Yes, she ended up dumping him. She'd worked herself up into such a state. She said he was blasé about being dumped and went willingly in the end. I told her to watch her back, not to trust him. She told me not to worry so much and that she had it all under control. I've seen my fair share of abuse victims around here, as you can imagine. Abusers tend to push the boundaries where they can, I see very few cases where they just up and leave. It's the control aspect that drives them on, isn't it?"

Carla nodded. "Yes, you're right. We've dealt with the same issues over the years. I don't suppose you know where we can find the ex?"

"He used to spend most of his spare time down at a snooker hall, the one in town, can't recall the name."

"Thanks, that's a help. What about his name, any idea?"

"Matt Allerton, I believe. Don't ask me where he's living now, though. He used to live with Kelly before she kicked him out. You need to speak to him, and quickly, before he tries to abscond."

Carla turned to Sara. "Would you mind ringing the station? Get a member of the team over to the snooker hall to pick him up if he's there."

Sara smiled, nodded and left the room. She rang the station and spoke to Craig. "Craig, we've obtained more information on the ex. I need you and Barry to go over to the snooker hall and pick him up. He's called Matt Allerton. Bring him in for questioning. You might want to try and find his address before you head off, just in case he's not at the snooker hall. With regard to the interview, I'll leave that in your capable hands. We might be tied up for a while here."

"Leave it with me, boss."

Sara ended the call and returned to the room. "All actioned. We'll bring him in for questioning, provided we can find him."

"Good, he can't be allowed to get away with this." The doctor nodded and wrung his hands.

"It's important for us to keep an open mind about this, for now. We might be doing the man an injustice," Carla stated. "What about around here? We're aware of how much hassle the staff always get from members of the public. Has anything untoward happened in the past week or so?"

The doctor paused to think for a moment. "I don't believe so. It's been relatively quiet on the aggression front since we employed the security guard."

"Good to hear. I bet it makes everyone feel safer having a professional heavy around."

"It does. Not that it's done Kelly any good. I still can't believe I'll never see her smiling face again. She was one in a million. I saw a great future ahead of us. I'd been keen on her for a while but knew she was seeing that jerk, therefore, I backed off. Why did I do that? We've missed out on so much. She used to come to work to forget all her woes; some days I would catch her looking thoroughly miserable. She seemed to brighten up the room when she entered it normally, so to see her in so much turmoil really touched me. Such a lovely lady."

"I'm sorry for your loss. Was there anyone else in her life who appeared to be causing her any stress, do you know?" Carla asked.

Sara poised her pen, ready to add to her notes, but the doctor shook his head. "I'm assuming that you're aware her mother has a drink problem?"

"Yes, we're aware. We've already spoken to her. She was very distraught when we visited her last night to break the news."

"I'm surprised by that. Maybe it'll make her sober up now."

"Or send her the other way," Carla remarked.

Sara nudged her knee with her own. Whether Carla thought that or not, it was always wise to keep opinions of that vein to yourself as an investigating officer.

Carla cleared her throat. "Did she have someone on the staff who she was close to? A female colleague we can possibly speak to?"

"Yes. Tania was one of her best friends. She's going to be distraught by the news. Do you want me to fetch her for you? You can use my office. I'll need to get back to work now, anyway, that is, if you've finished with me?"

"Yes, that would be great. Thanks for sparing us the time. We appreciate all the information you've given us."

He rose from his seat. "It was my pleasure. I'll be right back."

Sara watched him leave and close the door behind him and then whispered, "Juicy gossip right there."

Carla shrugged. "It happens, colleagues falling for one another."

Sara grinned, and her cheeks warmed. "Oops, yes, I had forgotten that's how you met Des. I wonder if their relationship might be the cause of some form of jealousy. After all, he's quite a catch. A dishy doctor, what's not to love?"

Carla chewed her lip. "Maybe. Should I go along those lines when I question the friend? Do you think she knew about their secret affair?"

"Only one way to find out. Don't come right out and ask her, my suggestion would be to ease into it."

"Will do."

There was a slight knock on the door which put an end to their conversation.

"Come in," Carla called.

A petite nurse entered the room. Her long black hair pulled into a ponytail hung down her back and bobbed as she walked around the desk to sit opposite them. "Hi, I'm Tania. Jackson told me you wanted to see me."

"Pleased to meet you. I'm DS Carla Jameson, and this is my partner, DI Sara Ramsey. Did he tell you why we asked to see you?"

She sighed. "No. To my knowledge, I haven't done anything wrong. Nothing to warrant the police calling at my place of work to question me. What's this about?"

Carla paused. Sara wondered if she should intervene, but then her partner found her voice again. "Tania, it is with regret that we have to share some bad news with you."

Tania's hands clenched together on the desk. "About what? Oh God, is it either of my parents? Are they all right?"

Carla raised a hand. "It isn't to do with your immediate family. However, this is concerning Kelly Pittman."

Tania's brow knitted, and her voice lowered. "What about her?"

"Sadly, she lost her life last night."

"What? You can't be serious. She was here, working alongside me

60

yesterday. We even made plans to go out at the weekend. This can't be true."

"I'm afraid it is."

"How? Was it an accident?"

"Not in the normal sense of the word. The investigation is still in its infancy. What I can tell you is that she lost her life close to home."

"I'm sorry, but I'm struggling to get my head around this. You're going to have to come right out and tell me how she died because my mind isn't working properly at the moment."

"The actual crime scene was at the base of her building, if that helps?"

"But she lives in a large block of flats... crime scene? I don't understand, what are you saying? That this wasn't an accident?"

"We don't believe so, no. We also discovered signs of a struggle inside her flat."

The creases in Tania's brow deepened. "I don't understand, are you telling me she managed to escape from someone who was trying to hurt her?"

Carla inhaled a breath. "What I'm telling you is that it would appear Kelly tried to fight off an attacker, but it proved pointless, and maybe she tried to escape out of the balcony, or maybe she was pushed to her death. It's the nitty-gritty details that we're struggling to work out."

Tania's mouth gaped open, and her head shook. She remained in that state for a few more seconds until the gravity of the situation became clear. "Are you telling me that she might have been murdered?"

"There's a distinct possibility. That's why we're here, to see if any of her colleagues can shed any light on what's been going on in her life lately. You being her best friend at work, you'd be ideal to fill in the gaps for us, if you can."

"I wish I could... bloody hell, I can't believe she's gone. Do you know who did this?"

"Not yet. Hence our need to interview her friends and colleagues. Do you know anyone who might possibly fit the bill?"

"Of what? Being a killer?" Tania retorted sharply.

"Anyone with a possible grudge against Kelly perhaps?"

"Only her ex, Matt. But, there again, I wouldn't necessarily put him down as a killer. Who knows these bloody days? Let's just say it's been an eye opener for me, transferring to A and E last year. I've seen my fair share of the damage people are capable of doing to others. Kindness and caring in the community appear to be things of days gone by, I can tell you. And don't get me started on the domestic abuse angle. She was abused by her ex, that's the only reason I put his name out there. I'm not the malicious sort, but he really is a piece of work. Wouldn't know how to speak to a woman nicely. What Kelly ever saw in him, I'll never know. I'm glad she found at least a smidgen of happiness before she died. Jackson worshipped her."

"You knew about their relationship?"

"Of course. She told me the second he asked her out. I was the one who encouraged her to go for it. He's an amazing man, very sensitive. She was waiting for another post to crop up in the hospital before she told everyone. I kept my mouth shut, of course. They were adorable together. He'll be really cut up about this."

"He seemed shocked by the news. Were they in love? How long had they been seeing each other, romantically?"

"Just over a month. Oh yes, she was head over heels in love with him. Spoke about the plans for their future together. Once she left the department, they were hoping to move in with each other and possibly get engaged."

"After only a month together?"

"Yes. Sometimes you instinctively know when a relationship is right."

Sara caught Carla glancing down at the ring sitting on her finger; she and Des had got engaged swiftly.

Carla then cleared her throat. "I suppose so. What about hassle from ex-girlfriends, were there any?"

"Jackson's exes, you mean?"

Carla nodded.

"He didn't really have any. Before he started showing an interest in

Kelly he wasn't bothered about dating. Kelly told me his last girlfriend had been over five years ago. I can believe that, too, he's devoted to his work. Spends most of his time here rather than having time off, or he did, until he started seeing Kelly. What a bloody loss she will be. Not only at work but as a friend. She was unbelievably kind, a pleasure to be around. Never had a bad word to say about anyone. She didn't even run that waste of space down when she ditched him."

"You're referring to Matt, I take it?"

"That's right. If he'd treated me the way he had her, I would have got my hands on one of those voodoo dolls and stuck a million pins in it."

Sara had to suppress a giggle at the image her mind conjured up.

"What about patients?" Carla asked. "Has Kelly ever had any dealings with irate patients?"

Tania snorted. "Haven't we all? Sometimes people strike out at us for merely doing our jobs. It can be utterly soul-destroying being on the frontline at times. And that was before the pandemic struck."

"We appreciate all that you do. It must be a thankless job most days," Sara chipped in.

"It is. Most nurses find it hard to take the strain occasionally, some even choose to jack the job in. We set out to help and heal people, but that is never enough for some folks."

"But having a security guard on duty now has eased the distress caused by the general public, yes?" Carla asked.

"Somewhat. You're still going to get the odd drunk lashing out when it is least expected of them."

"So nothing recently on that front?"

Tania shook her head. "Nothing is coming to mind, not lately."

"What about her friends, everything all right there? Or has she fallen out with anyone in the past couple of months?"

"I don't think so, not that I can think of. Like I said, she was a very placid type of person. The only blight in her life recently would have been her involvement with Matt. She seemed far more relaxed when he was out of her life. It was as if a heavy cloak had been lifted from her shoulders."

"Okay, I think we've heard enough now. I'll give you one of my cards. If you think about anything else you feel might be useful to the enquiry, please give me a ring."

"I will. What will happen now, with Kelly, I mean? Any idea when her funeral will take place?" Tania sniffled.

"It's far too early to say yet. Her mother is aware of her passing. The arrangements will be down to her to make, once Kelly's body has been released by the pathologist."

"Her mother? She couldn't organise a piss-up in a brewery, she'd be there, drinking herself to death, alone, rather than send out the invites to others. I've never met her, and Kelly didn't really mention her mother much, but I could tell it broke Kelly's heart to see her mother hitting the bottle heavily, especially after losing her father so suddenly a few months ago. That cut her to pieces, she was a real daddy's girl."

"It must have been tough on her to see her mother in such a state when she was crying out for her support after losing her father."

"Definitely. Families suck at times, don't they?"

"So true. Thanks for sparing the time to speak with us. Do you think it would be worth speaking to the other members of staff to see if they can fill in any gaps for us?"

Tania shook her head again. "I doubt it. I was her closest friend, and we worked the same shifts most days."

"Okay, thanks."

Sara closed the notebook, and the three of them stood and left the room. "Will you thank Jackson for letting us use his room?"

"I'll do that. I hope you solve the case soon and that we can lay Kelly to rest in a reasonable time."

"We're going to do our best. Take care," Carla said.

Sara and Carla headed back to the main entrance.

"You did well," Sara praised her partner.

"Thanks. I think the nerves showed at times but, basically, I enjoyed myself. Umm… is that the wrong term to use in the circumstances?"

"I get what you mean. So, what conclusions have you come to?"

They reached the car and got in. "That the spotlight is solely on the ex, at least for now, until something else comes our way to alter our minds. Do you agree?"

"I do. Let's head back to base, see if the boys have brought him in for questioning yet. First, I want to chase up Lorraine, keep on her back about the PM and the forensic results we're awaiting."

"You're thinking some of the blood at Kelly's flat might belong to the perp?"

"That's a distinct possibility. I don't want to be seen to be coming down heavy on the ex if the evidence fails to point in his direction."

"I get that. Do you want me to drive while you speak to Lorraine?"

Sara smiled and hopped out of the car. They switched seats, and she dialled Lorraine's number. "Hey, it's me. How are you doing?"

"Harassed as usual. Don't tell me you're ringing up to add to my misery!"

"Umm... sorry, yes. It sounds busy there, are you out and about?"

"Yep. Always busy. I've just arrived at another crime scene."

"A death?"

"Yep. Want to join me?"

"Why not? Where are you?"

"Rotherwas Industrial estate."

"We're just leaving the hospital now. Be there in around ten minutes, depending on the traffic situation, of course."

"See you soon. I'm outside unit fifty-eight."

"Is that significant?"

"Not sure just yet. We could do with some more bodies over here. We seem to be gaining a lot of spectators for some reason."

"I'll make the call, get some extra officers to attend."

"Thanks. I knew I could rely on you."

Sara pressed the End Call button and immediately rang the station to speak to the desk sergeant. "Hi, Jeff, it's DI Ramsey. I've just had a request from the pathologist to ask for more backup to attend the crime scene over at Rotherwas. Can you organise that for me?"

"Already actioned, ma'am. I have two cars en route. Forgive me for not getting in touch about the incident, I was umming and ahing about ringing you but thought better of it, given that you're already dealing with a murder case."

"We're on our way over there now, we'll take a look, see if we can handle both cases if no one else is available."

"That would be great. Thank you. We received a call from a mechanic at the garage down there. He arrived at work to find his colleague lying dead outside the workshop. There was no one else in the area."

"Okay, do we know how he died?"

"Unsure at present. The bloke who found him was pretty shaken up."

"Not to worry. I take it he's still at the scene?"

"Yes, I've told my lads to secure the area first, make it accessible to the techs, and then to take down the statement from the witness after that has all been implemented."

"Good job. Okay, we'll see you later."

Sara ended the call and leaned her head back. "Yet another death to look into. What is going on around here lately?"

"Do you think it's because the deaths appear in the press, others latching on to it, wanting their fifteen minutes of fame?"

Sara sat upright and glanced at her partner. "You think? That's a bit over the top, isn't it?"

"Nothing would surprise me any more."

"Maybe you have a point. Anyway, let's assess the crime scene when we get there and see if we want to take it on or not."

"That's unlike you, Sara. You usually jump at the chance to investigate an additional crime scene."

"Yeah, I know. But my head isn't really with it today, is it?"

"Sorry, I forgot. Do you want me to handle things when we get there?"

"I'm fine. Feeling far better than I did first thing at the hospital. Besides, that's what Mum wants me to do, work."

.   .   .

They arrived at the location to find several police cars on one patch of the car park and a couple of SOCO vehicles on another section. But the thing that surprised Sara the most was the number of spectators hanging around. "Jesus, what is wrong with people? We need to find out if anyone witnessed anything. If not, send the fuckers on their way, they could hamper the techs." Sara pointed at a couple of men standing at the rear of the crowd. "Shit! Even the press is in on the act. They're here early."

"Scavenging bastards," Carla grumbled.

They left the car on a mission. Sara nodded a brief hello at Lorraine and swept past her, aiming for the crowd. "Okay, would any witnesses to the incident step forward, please?"

A man in grey overalls dotted with oil patches raised his hand. "I'm the one who found him. I didn't see what happened, though."

Sara beckoned him. "If you can come with me, sir. Anyone else?"

"I saw what happened from my office over there." A woman pointed at one of the units across the road.

Sara smiled. "Can you come with me as well?"

"Sure. It was terrible."

"Anyone else?" Sara addressed the murmuring crowd. No one else raised their hand. "I'd appreciate it if you cleared the area then. The techs work more efficiently when they're given space to breathe. Thank you."

"Come now, Inspector Ramsey, that's bullshit, if ever I heard it," one of the journalists shouted back. The man appeared to have an obsession with her. He was always one of the first to show up at a crime scene, wanting to get in on the act early.

"Parker, are you causing mischief again? You've been warned about that in the past, I believe. Why don't you and your colleagues go about your business and wait for the press officer's announcement to come your way from the station?"

"Nah, we'll wait around. See what bits and pieces we can obtain from these good people after you've spoken to them."

"I could have you for intimidation, so tread carefully, Parker."

He waggled his eyebrows at her. "Bring it on, Inspector. You know I'm within my rights to be here."

He had her by the short and curlies and, judging by his smug expression, he knew it. *Bastard, I'm just in the right frame of mind to have a go at you, but doing it in front of a large crowd is going to make me look a right bitch.*

"Then it's entirely up to you. I'll be advising the witnesses not to speak with you."

He scowled. "You can't do that."

"Can't I? Maybe they won't want to speak to trashy journalists."

"Ooo... get you. Name-calling isn't usually a path you take, Inspector. Why change the habit of a lifetime?"

"I've wasted enough time as it is having a conversation with you, Parker. Let me and all the specialists around here get on with carrying out our jobs in peace."

"I ain't stopping them. Listen up, Inspector," he shouted louder. "The public have a right to know if there's a killer in their midst, I'm sure you'll agree."

"And if there is, the news should come from the evidence to back up such an impulsive claim, don't you agree?"

"There's nothing impulsive in the way I share news with the public, Inspector. I think you must be gravely mistaken there."

"Whatever, Parker. If you'll excuse me, I have work to do. I can't afford to spend my day hanging around, arguing the toss with the likes of you."

He tipped his head back and laughed. "I can sense when a copper is on the edge of an abyss."

Sara stormed over to where Carla was chatting with Lorraine and growled, "That fucker has gone too ruddy far this time. He gets on my tits at the best of times, but today... agh!"

"You're not having a good day, he's sensed that and pounced on your insecurities," Carla replied in a hushed voice.

Lorraine frowned, her gaze flicking between them. "What's going on?"

Sara sighed and closed her eyes. She peered over her shoulder to make sure there was no one unwanted lingering. "I found out this morning that my mum has cancer."

Shocked, Lorraine asked, "Shit! Is she going to be all right?"

The tears misted Sara's eyes, and she shook her head. "I can't talk about it, Lorraine. Sorry, nothing against you, but that bastard has just wound me up so much, if I say anything else I fear I'm going to break down and become a mess. He'd have a field day if I did that, wouldn't he?"

"All right. I won't push you. Don't forget I'm always at the end of the phone if you need to chat."

"I know. I appreciate your concern. I'll be all right once I get used to the idea. Until then, Carla is taking charge of the investigation, well, sort of, she's going to be interviewing friends and relatives and any witnesses who come our way, for now."

"I can totally understand your head not being in the right place. Just give me a shout if you need me to do anything above and beyond what I usually do during an investigation for you."

"You're incredible, Lorraine. Between Carla and the team, I think we have it covered. Although, things might change drastically if we take on this case as well. Do you have any spare suits in the van?"

"Sure. You know where they are. I'll get the guys to erect the tent to prevent the press and the rubberneckers from getting an eyeful of the victim. I covered him with a sheet as soon as I saw what we were up against."

"Glad you did that. Makes me sick the way people hang around when there's a dead body on show. Maybe they should be forced to attend a PM, that'd soon change their minds, arseholes."

Lorraine chuckled. "I'd be up for that. I'd intentionally make it gorier than usual."

Sara and Carla chuckled and then crossed the parking area to Lorraine's van, fished out two suits and stepped into them. They made their way back to Lorraine just in time to see the tent being erected. Sara couldn't hold back, she glanced in Parker's direction and poked her tongue out at him. He had the audacity to blow her a kiss. She shuddered under his gaze, and he laughed. *Fucking scumbag! You'll laugh at me once too often, moron.*

She turned her back on him, entered the tent and stood alongside Lorraine and Carla. Two techs were also inside, one taking samples around the body, the other taking the obligatory photos of the victim. "Any idea how he died yet, or is it too early?"

"I'm presuming the severe blows to his head are the cause."

The man's face was covered in blood, and there was a large patch on the ground beneath his head. Both his legs appeared to be broken as they were lying at odd angles.

"He took a battering by the look of things," Sara stated the obvious.

"I think we should leave Lorraine to it and see what the witnesses have to say," Carla suggested.

"Sounds like an excellent idea to me," Lorraine agreed. "Will you let me know what they say?"

"Will do," Sara called over her shoulder. She followed Carla out of the tent, and they crossed the car park to where the witnesses were standing, close to one of the other units. "We should speak to the woman first," Sara said out of the side of her mouth.

"I agree. The mechanic can wait. We need to find out how the incident occurred first. Do you want me to take the lead again?"

"Definitely. You did so well earlier."

They were within a couple of feet of the middle-aged woman by now. Carla and Sara produced their warrant cards.

"Thanks for agreeing to speak with us. I'm DS Jameson, and this is my boss, DI Ramsey. Perhaps we can start with you telling us what you actually saw."

"I'll try. I might end up a little tongue-tied, I'm out of my comfort zone talking to the police."

"It's fine. Take your time, there's no need for you to feel concerned," Carla reassured.

Sara prepared her notebook and pen.

The woman inhaled a large breath and tucked a stray lock of brunette hair behind her ear. "I was getting ready to start work. I came in early this morning, at around eight-thirty, I suppose. I'd just stopped by the staffroom to make a cup of tea and then sat down at my desk and booted up my computer. While that was going through the start-up process, I sipped my cuppa and a noise caught my attention. It was coming from this direction. I peered out of the window and saw one of those big motorbikes arrive. There were two people on the bike. They had a quick conversation with the man who died, and he started running towards the building. The bike revved up and drove at him. The person on the back of the bike was carrying what looked like a large metal bar—I might be mistaken about that, though. He struck the man's legs, and he dropped to the ground. The bike stopped, the person on the rear hopped off and began striking the man again and again." She swallowed noisily. "I was mesmerised by the events, I didn't want to watch but I was drawn to it, couldn't tear myself away from the gruesome scene."

"What happened then?" Carla prompted.

"The person got back on the bike, and it roared off. I left my office and raced over here to see if I could help the man. In the meantime, I think the other gentleman pulled into the car park, and he rushed over to see if he could help his work colleague. I should have called the police from my office, I know that now. I wasted valuable time. I never expected to come over here and find the man dead. I'm so confused. I keep reprimanding myself for not doing more to try to save him at the time. I suppose the fear of getting caught up in something so violent prevented me. I'm so sorry."

Carla smiled at the woman. "There's no need for you to apologise. My guess is that things escalated too quickly for you to react."

"Yes, yes, they did. That's correct. However, it will never change the fact that I might have been able to prevent it if I had tried harder. His poor family, how dreadful for them to be told of his death. Will you have to do that?"

"Unfortunately, that onerous task will be down to us, yes. Is there anything else you can tell us about the assailants?"

"No. They were in the usual get-up, all dressed in black leathers with those big helmets on. I couldn't even tell you what colour their hair was, let alone give you a full description of them."

"Did the bike have a number plate?" Carla asked.

"Not that I could see. I mean, it may have done, I did look but I couldn't see one. I thought it might have been because I was so far away."

"Sounds to me like they may have intentionally tried to cover their tracks. Please don't feel bad thinking you may have missed it. Can you tell me which direction they took when they left?"

"Yes, they went right, heading back into Hereford. Probably so they would get lost in the traffic which is heavy around that time of the morning."

Sara noted all the information down, her head whirling. On the road up ahead, in the direction they had come from, there were several available routes the assailants could have taken to avoid going back through the city centre. CCTV was going to be a godsend, as it always was during these types of cases.

"We'll look into it," Carla replied. "Is there anything else you'd like to add?"

The woman's mouth turned down at the sides, and she shook her head. "I don't think so. Graham might be able to help you more. Sorry, he's the other witness; we introduced ourselves. He was a work colleague of the dead man."

"Thanks very much, we'll have a quick chat with him. Would it be all right if we send an officer over to take a statement from you?"

"Of course. At work, or do you want my home address?"

"Either, it's up to you. On second thoughts, it depends how busy they are, so it might be better if you gave us your home address."

"It's thirteen Stockton Road, over by Dunelm."

"I know where it is, round the back there."

"That's it. I usually finish here at around five, I'll be home no later than six."

"Thanks for all your assistance. You may not think so, but I'm telling you, you've been a massive help today."

The woman blushed. "I do my best to be a considerate part of the community. If what I've told you here today helps you track down those monsters then that has to be an added bonus."

"Let's hope so. Thank you for speaking with us. Someone will be in touch with you soon."

"Can I go now?"

"You can." Carla looked over at the crowd. "I would suggest you go back to work that way, to avoid being questioned by strangers or any journalists lingering."

"Oh yes, I spotted them earlier. I'll steer clear, I prefer to stay out of the limelight, unlike some of the youngsters around today. Good luck with your investigation. I hope the victim gets the justice he deserves."

Carla nodded. "Thanks again for your help."

They waited until the woman was a few feet away, and then Sara said, "He was targeted, plain and simple."

"Yep, I was just about to say the same. Shall we see what his colleague has to say?"

"Why not? I doubt if he'll be able to add anything extra, but it has to be worth a shot."

The mechanic seemed understandably shaken up. He was leaning against the wall of one of the units.

"Hello, is it Graham?"

He nodded.

"I'm DS Jameson, and this is my partner, DI Ramsey. Are you up to answering a few questions?"

"I don't know much. I drove up, got out of the car and saw him lying there. He was my mate. A decent guy. Why would someone kill him? It doesn't make any sense to me."

"That's what we intend to find out. You arrived after the incident took place, I gather?"

"That's right. I wish I'd arrived five minutes earlier, I could have fended the fuckers off, at least tried to, anyway."

"You knew the victim well, I take it?" Carla asked.

"Yes, Adam and I have run this place together for around five years, give or take a few months. You should know that I rang his wife after I called nine-nine-nine, so she's aware of what's happened. I'm sorry, I should've thought about it more before I made the call. The news destroyed her, as you'd expect. She wanted to come down here, to be with him. I persuaded her not to. They've got a two-year-old daughter. I thought she should stay at home with the girl."

"It's fine. Thanks for letting us know, we'll pay her a visit after we've finished here. Did Adam ever mention if he was in any kind of trouble?"

"No. As far as I knew, he kept his nose clean. He was either here, working alongside me, or at home with Dawn and Angel, their little girl. He was devoted to the pair of them. Put in the extra hours around here when needed, worked his day off when it was necessary, all to make their lives so much better."

"He sounded a genuinely nice man. I'm sorry for your loss," Carla replied. "You're no doubt aware that the attack was carried out by two people riding a motorbike."

"Yes, the woman who witnessed the attack told me."

"Do you know anyone who rides a bike? Have either you or Adam serviced a bike recently, or is that a specialised need?"

"No, bikes don't generally come our way. It was a shock to hear that the attack had happened in the daylight. Who would do that? They must have some balls to even contemplate getting caught."

Carla looked up at the unit. "Do you have cameras on site?"

"We've never really felt the need to have them installed, until now. It's the first thing I'm going to do when I open up." He shook his head. "Jesus, what a way to go. Poor bloke. He didn't deserve this, I'm telling you. You couldn't meet a more decent chap."

"Do you know much about his friends and acquaintances?"

"Not really. Since the baby came along, he's not been out much."

"What about his family? Mother, father, brothers or sisters? Did he ever mention them?"

"Of course he did. They all come here to get their cars serviced, he always gave them a discount—those he couldn't fix at home, that is. What are you asking? That you think his family might be behind the attack?"

"No, not at all. Maybe a member of his family has taken the wrong road over the years and someone has decided to send them a warning message."

Graham's brow furrowed. "Are you insane? What, by showing up here and killing Adam?"

Carla faced Sara and closed her eyes. It was clear her partner was struggling.

Sara took over. "What my partner is getting at is right, we've seen this type of thing happen numerous times over the years."

"Bloody hell. If that's the case, then there must be some sick fuckers walking, or should I say driving, around Hereford."

"It's possible. Can you give us his address?" Sara asked.

"I'll have to get it from the office. I know the road but can't remember the number off the top of my head."

He searched his pocket for a set of keys and unlocked the small door to the unit. "Do you want to step inside?"

"Thanks. We'll follow you in." Sara waited until Graham had gone through the door then turned to face Carla. "What's up with you?"

"I shouldn't have let my mouth run away with me."

"You're making a mountain out of a molehill, love. Give yourself a good talking-to and jump back in. You were doing well up until that point."

Carla heaved out a weary sigh. "Was I? I'm having to think on my feet, none of this is coming naturally to me, not like it does to you."

"Who says it does? I struggle to keep things fresh with every single interview. Don't give up now, not after a few hours, Carla."

"All right. Is that the lecture over and done with now?"

Sara flicked her partner's arm. "Cheeky mare. I never lecture. I offer good sound advice."

"Of course you do." Carla chuckled.

They entered the building and closed the door behind them. The smell of engine oil was the first thing to hit Sara's nostrils. She hated the smell, always had done. She cleared her throat and hurried into the office where the smell dulled but lingered faintly.

"Here it is. Number seventy-six Turnpike Road, Eign Hill. He's got a small terraced house down there. Only had it a few years. They've been saving like crazy to pay off the mortgage. It's been a struggle, what with the bloody pandemic rearing its head. I suppose we're all struggling financially, aren't we?"

"Very true, what with all the prices skyrocketing," Carla said, back on her game. "Is there anything else you can tell us? Have either of you had a run-in with a customer lately, maybe about a large bill, that sort of thing?"

"No. We're not one of these garages who do the work first and bill the customer later, we always make them aware of any excess charges they might incur before we start the work. We've been burnt before, you see. A case of once bitten…"

"I can understand that. Okay, I think we've covered everything here. I'm afraid SOCO will be around for the next few days, so you might want to ring your customers and postpone any appointments you have booked in."

"Great. Not what I wanted to hear, what with business being slow right now. But hey, I guess it's to be expected I suppose with Adam losing his life." He tutted, and his head dipped.

"Again, we're sorry for your loss. We'll leave you to it. Here's one of my cards. If you either think of anything or have any unexpected visitors, please contact me ASAP."

"Jesus, are you telling me you think these guys might come back and have a go at me?"

Carla raised her hands. "No, sorry, I wasn't suggesting anything of the sort. All I'm asking is that you remain vigilant, just in case."

He blew out a frustrated breath and glanced around him. "I will. I'll ring my customers to postpone things and then go home. You reckon I'll be safe then?"

"I'm sure this was a one-off incident. Try not to be too concerned."

"If you say so, but it's going to be easier said than done. My wife is going to go out of her freaking mind. How am I supposed to console her? No, don't answer that, it was a rhetorical question."

"All I can say is that it seems to me that Adam may have been specifically targeted. We just need to find out why."

"I can't help you. I wish I could but I've racked my brains and can't come up with a single reason why someone would come here and bump him off."

"Not to worry. Give me a ring if anything comes to mind later."

"I'll be sure to do that. I'm going to lock up and go home now, if that's okay?"

"Of course."

Sara and Carla left the garage.

"How did I do?" Carla asked, sounding a tad insecure.

"You did fine. Maybe you let the interview go on a little too long, especially when it was obvious he didn't know anything."

"Ah, yes. The quick in-and-out option would have been better, although, in my defence, he was very shaken up, so my thinking was that his mind would have likely been all over the place, and continuing to stay with him might have jolted something, eventually."

Sara inclined her head. "One way of looking at it. You did nothing wrong, partner, not really. Come on, let's have a quick chat with Lorraine before we visit the wife. She's likely to be a mess when we turn up."

They walked across the car park again.

"Not ideal, her already knowing that her husband is dead. Nothing we can do about that now."

"Inspector Ramsey," a voice that made her cringe surfaced from the crowd.

Sara did her best to ignore Parker, the pest of a journalist.

"Found out who the killer is yet, have you?"

She clenched her fists, ensuring she wasn't tempted to give him the finger in front of the members of public still in attendance.

"Ignore him," Carla leaned in and whispered.

"I'm doing my best, but it isn't easy, I can assure you."

Lorraine was searching for something in the back of her van. She heard what the journalist had shouted and spun around to glare at him.

"Don't retaliate, Lorraine, he isn't worth it," Sara warned.

"How do you put up with jerks like that?"

Sara sighed. "Sometimes it comes with the territory. I tend to ignore them when I can. I must admit, he's being a prize fucker today."

"Arsehole," Lorraine mumbled. "How did you get on with the witnesses?"

Sara intentionally kept her voice low. "The woman saw all that happened. The victim didn't stand a chance. Two people showed up on a bike. One pulled out a large bar and started attacking the victim's legs, brought him to the ground, then hit him over and over until he was dead."

"Yikes. That poor man. Is the woman all right, after witnessing such an horrific attack?"

"Surprisingly, yes. More together than I would have been in her shoes. She came over to see if she could help after the bike left the area, that's when Graham showed up. He owns the garage with the victim, Adam Casey. According to him, they've had no bother in the last few months. We asked if he knew anything about Adam's life and if he'd been in any form of trouble, but he said no, that he was a family man. Spent every evening with his wife and their two-year-old daughter. So, nothing untoward there. We'll need to do the normal digging into the financial side of things, but I'm not hopeful after chatting with his partner."

"It's an odd one."

"It is. Between you and me, and I know I shouldn't be saying this but, I can't see us spending a lot of time on this investigation compared to the other case we're dealing with right now. I'll put a couple of officers on this one and keep the bulk of the team on the Kelly Pittman case."

"Makes sense to me," Carla affirmed. "Of course, once we've spoken to the wife, we might have to rethink that."

"Agreed," Sara said. "Do you need us any more, Lorraine?"

"No, not at all. You get off. I'll keep in touch with regard to both cases."

"I don't envy you, having two imminent PMs on your plate."

"It is what it is. Speak later." Lorraine took the bag she'd collected and dipped back inside the tent.

"We need to try and move this crowd on, without the hecklers getting involved," Sara grumbled.

"Good luck with that one. I think I'd rather get out of here and leave it to uniform to deal with."

"You're right. Let me have a brief chat with them, and then we'll shoot over to see the vic's wife."

Carla went back to the car, and Sara, true to her word, had a quick conversation with the uniformed officers doing their best to control the onlookers. She told them to give it another ten minutes before dishing out threats they would be arrested for interfering with an investigation. *That should shut Parker up, tosser!*

4

*A*dam Casey's family lived on one of the new estates. He and his wife owned a terraced house towards the rear, away from the main road. When they pulled up outside the property, his wife immediately looked out of the front room window. She had her daughter sitting on her hip.

Sara offered up a smile and waved at the woman. "Here goes. This is down to you again, Carla. I'll jump in if you need me to."

"Thanks... I think."

The front door opened while they were halfway between the car and the house. "Are you the police?" the woman asked, eyeing them guardedly.

Carla and Sara produced their warrant cards. Mrs Casey studied each one carefully and then took a step back, allowing them to enter her home.

"Would you like us to take off our shoes?" Sara asked. "I've got a new-build myself."

"It's up to you. I'm not that bothered, it's not as if it's wet out there. Come into the lounge."

They followed her into the first room on the right where she put her daughter in a playpen in the far corner. "Now you be a good little girl for Mummy, I'll be right here, talking to these nice ladies."

The child pounced on a couple of the toys and started banging one against the other. Mrs Casey swapped the toys for teddies and rolled her eyes as she walked back to them. "Always tough, juggling what to give her. Please take a seat."

"Thank you." Sara left it to Carla to start the interview. "Mrs Casey, Graham told us that he rang you about your husband. We just want to offer you our condolences."

"Thank you. Please, call me Dawn. It's the hardest phone call I've ever received. Do you know why it happened?" Tears emerged and slid down her cheeks.

Sara sensed the woman had been trying to hold things together for her daughter's sake, knowing how sensitive children were, picking up on any kind of stress and anxiety.

"All we know is that a motorbike appeared with two people on board and one of them attacked your husband with a metal pole. They drove off soon after. Do you have any idea who the attackers might be?"

Dawn shook her head and sniffled. She withdrew a tissue from her sleeve and wiped the tears away. "No, I don't have a clue. As far as I know, my husband was well liked. He got on with most people. He was an easy-going kind of man. I still can't get my head around why someone would do this to him." She glanced over at her daughter, playing happily. "She will never really know him, not the way I knew him. He adored her. He told me last night he was the happiest he'd ever been, and it showed. We shared a lot of family time together. He was never late home from work. He was reliable to a fault. I couldn't have asked for a better husband."

"I'm so sorry this has happened to you and your daughter. I take it your husband wasn't dealing with any problems at the moment."

"Nothing. We were financially stable, as well as we could be, after the pandemic. I think every business suffered during those dark days. He has regular customers at the garage so is always busy there. And he used to come straight home from work to be with us, whereas other men find an excuse to stop off at a pub. He never did that. I insisted he should go sometimes, but he was having none of it. His life was so much better now he had me and Angel to come home to, that's what he used to regularly tell me. We were very much in love. I don't think I'll ever find such a caring man again. Why has someone come along and destroyed our lives like this?" Her tears flowed faster.

"Can I get you a drink?" Sara asked.

Dawn waved the suggestion away and blew her nose. "No, I'll be fine. I had a drink before you got here. Sorry, I should have asked, can I get you one?"

"No, we're fine," Sara replied.

Carla and Sara shared a look. Sara gave a brief nod, giving Carla the go-ahead to proceed cautiously.

"At the moment, we have very little to go on to begin the investigation. After speaking to you and his partner, we're struggling to make sense of things. Is there anything that you can tell us? Any suggestion that your husband might have fallen out with one of the neighbours recently, anything along those lines?"

"No, there's nothing at all. Let me rephrase that, nothing that I'm aware of. He wasn't the type to keep secrets from me. He would have told me if he'd faced any trouble or danger lately."

"Could he have owed money to someone?"

She swallowed and shook her head. "No, not at all. We were financially stable. We don't go out much and tend to save a lot of Adam's wages. We're... or should I say, we had plans to have another baby in the near future and we had just started discussing moving to a bigger house." The sadness descended.

"I'm so sorry," Carla said sympathetically. "What about his brothers or sisters? Could they have been in any form of trouble?"

"What if they had? You think the person would have taken it out on Adam? Killed him?"

Carla shrugged. "It's something we need to look into. Can you give us his siblings' names and addresses?"

"I'm telling you that you've got this all wrong. I'll get their details for you but I doubt if it will help."

She left the room, and Carla faced Sara for approval.

"Stop doubting yourself. You're doing fine."

Carla leaned towards her. "Is there something else I should be asking?"

"No, there's nothing you've missed. We'll get the siblings' details and leave her to it. Before we leave, just ask if she wants us to call anyone to come and sit with her. I get the impression that she's putting on a brave face. I think the more questions you ask, the more it's likely to hit home and affect her."

"Okay, I'll bear that in mind. But I'm doing okay so far?"

Sara chuckled. "Yes, you're doing fine. Stop stressing about it."

The door opened, and Dawn came in holding her mobile phone. She looked up one contact and handed her phone to Sara to jot down the information before moving on to the next family member. "That's it. Cheryl and Russ, his sister and brother. Unless you want his parents' address as well?"

"We might as well. Do you all get along?"

"Yes, from day one they accepted me into their family. We spend as much time together as we can. Christmas is always a blast… or it used to be. All of us turning up at his parents' house, mucking in with the dinner, never leaving it to one person. They're a true family unit, not a bad penny amongst them."

"Thank you, that's good to know. We won't keep you. Is there anyone you'd like us to ring? Perhaps someone should be with you, in case the reality of the situation hits home after we leave."

"No, I'll call my mother if things get too tough to handle. I think I'd rather be by myself with Angel for now. I can pick her up for a cuddle without anyone asking me constantly if I'm all right. Don't get me wrong, my heart is breaking and exceedingly painful at the moment, I don't think that's going to change anytime soon, but it's my responsibility to hold it together for our daughter's sake. I don't want to cause her any more anxiety than is necessary. I suppose those are my mothering instincts kicking in."

"You're right," Carla responded. "I'm going to leave you my card, don't hesitate to contact me if you think of any questions after we've left."

"Umm... I do have one... when can I see him, to say goodbye?"

"I'll have a word with the pathologist, she'll get in touch with you as soon as the post-mortem has been performed."

Dawn's head fell, and fresh tears trickled. "Oh God, the thought of him being cut open..."

Carla nodded. "I'm sorry. It's a necessity when a suspicious death has occurred."

"How dreadful. Will I see the cuts when I visit him? I'm sorry if that sounds a dumb question."

"It's not. No, your husband will have been stitched up and his body will be covered by a sheet at the viewing. It's quite serene. Most people feel anxious before the visit but are grateful to the staff at the mortuary afterwards, for making the experience an easy process to go through. If that makes sense?"

"It does. Thank you. I can't say I'm looking forward to it, but I feel better knowing what to expect now. Is there anything else you need from me?"

"No. That's all for now. Maybe we should take your phone number just in case anything crops up during the investigation that we might need to run past you."

Dawn gave them the number, and Sara jotted it down.

She stood to show them out. They shook hands at the door.

Sara smiled and said, "Please, don't be afraid of seeking help over the coming days. Grief can affect people in different ways."

"Thank you. I'll keep an eye on my emotions and do the right thing for me and my daughter. Please, do your best to find Adam's killers."

"You have our promise. Take care of yourself and your daughter."

She closed the door, and they walked back to the car.

Carla sighed once she was seated. "That was tough. Her reactions weren't what we are used to at all."

"Granted. Not every person handles grief by the book. It's a personal choice. She has her child to consider. I can understand where she's coming from. I think it will hit her hard in a few hours."

"If it does, I hope she reaches out to someone and doesn't try to cope on her own. What a pig of a situation. We're no further forward. Why would anyone attack and kill someone like that for no reason?"

Sara chewed on her lip for a few seconds as she thought. "None of this is making sense to me. We have two complex investigations to deal with now."

"Where do we go from here?"

"We should visit Adam's family, if only to rule them out. Maybe they'll be able to tell us more."

"You think he was keeping a secret from his wife?"

Sara shrugged and started the engine. "Who knows? It's not like we have anything else to go on, is it?"

Carla leaned her head against the window. "Frustratingly, no."

hree hours later, Sara and Carla returned to the station. They had questioned Adam's distraught parents and his brother and sister, only to come away feeling even more frustrated. *What the fuck are we up against here? There are no contributing factors as to why he should have been murdered. So where do we go from here?*

Sara gathered the team together and went through what they'd learned regarding the new crime scene. "Marissa and Christine, I'd like you both to team up and handle the second case. We've done the necessary legwork on it, all you need to do now is the normal process at this end. You know, check into the victim's background, see if he had a record, and most of all check the financial side of things. Let me know when you've completed all that and we'll put our heads together to decide what we do next."

"Any time limit on getting the results back to you?" Christine asked.

"The earlier the better, without putting yourselves under too much stress."

Both ladies nodded.

"As for the rest of us, we all need to focus on the Kelly Pittman case." She noted that Barry and Craig were missing; it had slipped her mind to seek them out. Her head really wasn't with it today. Hardly surprising, considering her mother's illness. "Have the boys reported back yet? I take it they're still questioning the ex-boyfriend downstairs?"

"Not yet," Jill replied.

"Okay. I'll take a wander down there and see how they're getting on. We're going to need to hear what the ex has to say first before we can continue. I'll go now. As you were, team."

"Want me to come?" Carla asked as if sensing Sara wasn't really with it.

"No, I don't need babysitting," she snapped. Sara regretted her choice of words instantly. She glanced at her partner who appeared wounded and mouthed an apology.

Carla smiled and nodded her acceptance.

Sara left the incident room and made her way downstairs. The light was on outside Interview Room One. She tapped on the door and stuck her head into the room. "Can I have a quick chat, DC Thomas?"

Barry joined her in the hallway. He leaned against the wall and placed his hands on his knees. "It's hard work. Maybe the hardest interview I've ever had the misfortune of conducting."

"Oh, why?"

He straightened up, his gaze meeting hers, and said, "If I hear those two confounded words once more, I think I'm going to scream like a five-year-old."

Sara sniggered. "That old chestnut. I suppose his solicitor has instructed him to go down that route. Do you want me to have a shot at him?"

Barry considered her question for a while and then shook his head. "Nope, I'm not a defeatist."

Sara patted him on the shoulder. "Good man. Has he given you anything at all?"

"His name and address, nothing we didn't already know."

"What's your gut telling you from his reactions to the questions you're asking?"

"That's a tough one. If I had to put a hundred quid on the table, I'd say he didn't do it. Yes, he's guilty of being a grade-A tosser, but I fear that's all it amounts to."

"That's disappointing. Okay, stick with it for another hour or so and then call it a day if you feel you're not getting any further with him."

"If that's what you want, boss. I'll get back to it."

Barry smiled and reentered the room. Sara drifted back upstairs and sat in her office for the next couple of hours going through the paperwork that had lain untouched for the past few days. It was no good, though, her focus lay elsewhere, so much so that she buckled and rang the hospital to see how her mother was.

She was put through to the ward. "Hello, I'm Elizabeth Beaumont's daughter, can you tell me if she's okay? Sorry to be a pest. I'm at work, you see, and can't get her out of my mind."

"You were here earlier, weren't you? With your sister."

"Yes, that's right. Mum was going for further tests."

"She's had an MRI scan and several other tests. I'm afraid we won't have the results back for a few days."

Sara sighed. "I suspected you might say that. I'm sorry to bother you."

"Hey, there's no need for you to say that. You care, it's only natural for you to want to know how your mother is doing. Feel free to ring anytime, if it helps to put your mind at rest. What I can tell you is that she's comfortable. Since coming back on the ward, she's slept quite a lot. I was there when she woke up and reached for your father's hand. It's clear they love each other very much."

Sara coughed to clear the lump that had formed. "It's going to hit Dad so hard, you know, when the time comes. Correction, it's going to destroy us all."

"I can imagine. What we tend to tell the family members in these situations is to cling on to the time they have left together. No one knows how long that is in most cases, it depends on the individuals concerned and how progressive the cancer is. I can confirm that your mother, although she's very tired, has a determination about her that I haven't seen in a long while. She's aware of how much you all love her."

"We do. She's the mainstay of our family, the true matriarchal force to be reckoned with, she always has been and always will be. When the time comes, we're going to be lost without her."

"I can understand that from the brief time I have known her. Stay strong."

"I'm doing my very best."

"You're doing the right thing, continuing to work and not dwelling on your mother's condition. In my experience, sitting at home, simply worrying about things, can bring a person down very quickly. Most people feel guilty going back to work, to me, it's the perfect medicine for family members."

"I'm here, but I have to tell you, I'm not functioning fully. I'm usually able to cope with all manner of stresses and strains as I'm an inspector in the police, however, I'm in charge of a super team of officers who are making life a whole lot easier for me right now."

"Good to hear. You need to take a step back to reassess what's going on around you now and again. My father was an inspector up in Birmingham, he retired around five years ago. He still misses the daily routine, even though he thought he detested it at the time."

"It's a double-edged sword for sure. So much satisfaction when we solve a case, however, at the same time, the paperwork involved in solving each investigation can be a logistical nightmare to wrap up and can often take weeks for us to complete."

"He used to say the same. The paperwork side of things used to be like torture to my father."

"Anyway, I'd better get back to it. Will you tell my parents I called and send them both my love?"

"I'll be sure to do that. Take care. Try not to punish yourself too much."

"I'll do my very best."

Sara ended the call. Not long after there was a knock on the door, and Carla appeared with a welcome cup of coffee.

"You read my mind. Thanks, partner."

"I heard you on the phone. Were you checking up on your mother?"

"Take a seat. Yes, she seems a little tired at the moment. She's been for an MRI scan and she's resting now."

"Ah, that will give them the answers they're seeking, and you guys, too. How's your dad holding up?"

"I had a chat with the nurse, I hate ringing people's mobiles when they're visiting someone in hospital, anyway, the nurse didn't really mention how Dad was and I forgot to ask. I hope he's all right. He's there with her, that's all that matters. It's further down the line that I'm worried about."

"I know. It's going to be a difficult time for all of you in the weeks to come. I want to assure you that I will always be here for you, whether you want to vent or if you need a shoulder to cry on."

"Thanks, Carla, that means a lot to me."

She shrugged. "It's the least I can do after all you've done for me over the past year or so. See it as payback." Carla grinned and raised her cup.

Sara picked up her cup and smiled at her partner. "We make a fantastic team, not sure if I'd be coping right now if you didn't have my back. I'll always appreciate you for stepping up for me today, Carla."

Carla's eyes watered. "God, don't start me off."

"I won't. Right, back to work. Have Barry and Craig come back yet?"

"Yes, just. No good. It was a total waste of time speaking with him. Well, from what I can gather it was a one-sided conversation."

"So I heard. Any form of alibi to check out?"

"Yes. Surprise, surprise, he told them that he was down at the snooker hall at the time of her death."

"Easy to check out, I suppose. What was his reaction to Kelly's death?"

"I asked Barry the same question. He said that Allerton simply shrugged. He showed little emotion either way."

"Heartless bastard. Still, aware of his track record of abusing her, I don't suppose we should be that surprised, should we?"

"I said the same."

"So, where does that leave us?"

"You want the obvious answer?" Carla replied.

"What about the house-to-house enquiries with regard to the neighbours? Did anyone see anything? A stranger coming out of the flat? Someone on that floor they didn't recognise?"

"Nothing. A couple of them heard a scream but didn't think anything of it at the time. Apparently, that's nothing new for around there."

"Shit! We've really got our backs against the wall with two investigations to handle now, not just one."

"Makes you question whether we should have taken the second case on or not, it means our resources are going to be stretched."

Sara inclined her head. "You think we should have ignored the second case and concentrated all of our efforts on the Kelly Pittman case, is that it?"

Carla blew out a breath and held up her upturned hands. "I don't know what I'm trying to say. I guess it's the frustration talking."

"Don't give up now. Let me finish doing this crap, and we'll put our heads together about both cases, deal?"

Rising from her seat and taking her cup with her, Carla smiled. "That's a deal. Good luck."

A few hours later, Carla welcomed Sara back into the fold with the news that a motorbike had been found dumped in the River Wye.

5

*M*ona tore up the stairs to confront Warren, not for the first time over the past few days. "When are you going to start fucking listening to me?"

Warren was stretched out on the bed, flicking through one of his auto magazines. He glanced her way and rolled his eyes. "Here we go again. Didn't you hear me? I said I needed space from all the aggravation you're dishing out."

"That's tough. If I've told you once, I've told you a million times over, I want out of this crippling situation."

"Yeah, I heard you, every single time, and I keep telling you, there's no bloody way out of this, for either of us."

Mona raced across the room, flying at him with clenched fists, striking his arms and face over and over. "Why? Why did you frigging get me into this mess? I warned you not to get involved, but you wouldn't listen to me. You treat me like a dumb bitch most of the time, but I sometimes wonder if I'm the brains in this relationship."

He grabbed both of her hands in his and tipped his head back to let out a laugh. "Stop wondering, you're not. Let's face it, without me you'd still be stripping in that seedy club, surrounded by mauling, desperate men."

Her mouth screwed up as her temper rose. "Why, you fucking scumbag. How dare you? That job put a roof over my head and kept me off the streets for years."

"Barely. Before I came along to save you, you lived in a squat with dozens of other druggies. I cleaned you up and put you on the right path, even found you the job working at the bowling alley, but that didn't last long. Since then, you've been bleeding me dry, sat around here on your arse all day. I wouldn't mind, but the place is a sodding tip. Ever heard of a duster or a vacuum cleaner?"

She tried to free her hands from his grasp, but he squeezed them tighter. "You fucking heap of shit. You think you're so much better than me. You want to take a look in the mirror sometime, big man. You'd be surprised what you see."

He laughed again. Their feisty encounter drew to a close as soon as his mobile rang. "Damn, pack it in, this is serious. He's on the phone again. Sit there and keep quiet." Warren picked up the burner phone sitting alongside his regular mobile and sucked in a steadying breath. "Hello." He put the phone on speaker so Mona could hear.

"How's it going?"

"We've managed to track down two of them."

"And the outcome?" the impatient goon asked.

"Both dead. One case has been on the media, we're waiting for the other one to appear. I reckon it'll be on the news this evening."

"Good. But the boss wants more. He reckons you should have punished half of them by now. He's told me to heap the pressure on you."

"*What*? There's no need for that. I told you we'd get the job done. It's all in the planning process, you've got to allow us time to make the kills, man."

"Something ain't sitting right with the boss. He's told me to issue a warning, so here I am."

"Okay, I'm hearing you, but I can't be out there doing what you ask during the day, I've got work. If I slacken off there, folks are going to start asking questions. Is that what you want?"

"Fuck, man, it ain't any of my business. You need to learn what the boss wants, the boss gets. So you'd better get on with it and knuckle down."

"Or else? I'm getting sick and tired of these threats," Warren shouted.

"Is that so? Well, you've got two options, either carry out the jobs dished out to you or..."

"Or?" Warren snapped back, the colour draining from his cheeks.

Mona gulped noisily and clung to his hand. She knew it was a risk getting involved, but Potter and his boss had them by the short and curlies.

"I have to spell it out to you? Are you for frigging real? All right, let's just say we've done our research on your family and now have a dossier on them. Two of my guys have been following them around for months now, we know their routines and are willing to strike, when it suits us. As I see it, you've got one option to prevent that from happening: complete the task you've been given. Simples, right?"

Warren ran his tongue across his dry lips. Mona clenched his hand tighter, showing her support.

"Okay, we'll do as you ask. The third one will be dealt with today."

"Make it a key part of the puzzle, if you get my drift?"

"You want me to kill the main man?"

"Yep. The boss wants you to show him you've got the balls to carry this off."

"Umm... won't that go against us with the cops?"

Potter laughed. "We couldn't give a toss. The filth in this town are useless anyway, so what does it matter?"

"I'm putting my career on the line if we up the ante now. The arrangement was that you'd leave the decisions up to me."

"*The arrangement was...*" Potter mimicked. "Listen here, dickhead, you do *what* we say and *when* we say it, got that? The boss is pulling your strings, you'd be wise not to forget it."

"All right. I hear you. I'm just voicing my objection to upping our plans, that's all."

"You can do what you fucking like, it ain't going to matter. You should know by now, what the boss wants, he gets," the goon repeated.

"He's made that perfectly clear from the outset."

"So, I can report back to him that you're on the case and that the victims will be dropping like flies over the coming few days, yes?"

"If you insist."

"We do. You know the consequences if you go back on your word. My advice would be, don't do it."

Warren stared at Mona's shocked expression and ended the call.

She shot off the bed and walked the length of it, up and down, not saying a word, her head spinning out of control until it finally sank in what they were up against.

He held out a hand to her. "Come here."

"No. I don't want to be near you. What have you got us into here? At first, when you told me what they expected, I thought it was a joke. Shit, I've never been more wrong in my life. Fuck, fuck, fuck. I want out of this."

"Impossible. The only way we're going to be able to do what they say is if we continue to work as a team."

"Weren't you listening? They want it all done and dusted within days. We can't kill that many people... more to the point, I can't. I want out. Now."

He tore off the bed and latched on to the top of her arms. "It's not going to happen. We're in this together, until the end."

Her mouth gaped open for a second or two, and then she asked, "What happens at the end? When we've carried out their dirty work, you think that's going to be the end of it? Do you?"

"Of course it will."

She wrenched her arms out of his firm grasp. "How bloody naïve are you? You're going to be his bitch for the rest of your life."

"No, correction, we're a team. You're deep in it as much as me, for your information."

"Fuck you. If I could walk away tomorrow, I'd do it in a heartbeat."

Warren roared again. "And where would you go? Back to stripping and dosed up with drugs? You really want that?"

"It's better than the alternative. They've got this hold over us for life now, so I'm willing to take my chances if necessary."

"Fuck off, like shit you are! As usual, you're letting that mouth of yours run away with you. The mouth goes into action but the soul isn't willing, that's right, isn't it?"

She took a step forward and slapped his smug face. "You think you're so damn smart, you fuckwit. If that was the case, we wouldn't be up to our necks in shite. Remind me what I ever saw in you?"

"A ticket out of the hellhole you were living in. Screw you, babe. Enough of going around in circles. We need to get our act together and start planning out the next few days."

"Or what? Risk the morons going after our families?"

"You heard him. They're not the type to make idle threats."

"Well, it'll be your family at risk."

He punched her in the stomach.

She doubled over, winded. "What the fuck was that for?"

"Keep your smart mouth shut. I can easily give them the details of your family, forget that at your peril, bitch."

She pulled herself upright and touched noses with him. "Don't think I'm scared of you, because I ain't, got that?"

"Whatever. We need to stop this and get to work. It's almost five now, we can make two hits tonight, if we think smart."

"According to you, you're the bloody smart one, so you'd better put your thinking cap on because, by the sound of it, Potter and his boss are going to want that kill list completed ASAP." She groaned and hit her thigh with a clenched fist. "How the fuck did we get into this?" she complained for the umpteenth time.

"You know how. That's not the issue here. Come on, we're wasting time discussing the whys and wherefores, we need to form a plan for the next few days."

"And what if I told you I've had enough? What then?"

He reached for her. She took a step back. He then pounced on her and firmly gripped her around the throat. "You really want to find out?"

She kicked out and wriggled out of his grasp. "Don't push me, Warren."

Tilting his head, he said, "Sounds like an 'or' should be at the end of that sentence."

"I'll leave it there... for now. Just remember, you sleep well at night and I don't."

"Meaning?"

She smirked. "I'll leave that to your imagination to sort out."

*J*ust over an hour later, they hit the road. They knew who their target was going to be, the dilemma was how to nab the man. They parked the stolen car they had acquired earlier outside the man's office building and waited patiently for him to exit. They knew he was still at work. Warren had called the office, pretending to be a maintenance man, and spoken to his personal assistant. She'd told him that the two of them were working late but would be leaving within the next ten minutes.

Seconds later, the target and his assistant left the building. They both climbed into their respective cars and drove off in opposite directions at the first set of lights.

"Are you ready for this?" Warren asked.

"I doubt if anyone can be ready for murder, it just happens... er, what am I saying? See, you've done this to me, I no longer make sense when I open my damn mouth."

"Then shut the fuck up."

"Charming." Mona sulked.

Warren followed the car through the city centre and out towards Belmont where they knew the target lived.

"When are you going to do it? Make the hit?"

Warren briefly faced her and smiled. "Soon enough. I'm biding my time." He turned his attention back to the road ahead.

"Great, let me know what you decide and when you decide to do it, won't you?"

"Don't worry, you'll be the first to know."

By now, the farther they got out of town, the more the traffic had eased in their favour. They were the only two cars on the road now. Warren flashed his lights at the target's car. The man eyed him in his rear-view mirror and pulled into a lay-by a few feet ahead.

"Get ready. I'll tie him up and then you can get out of the car."

"Here? But it's too open."

"It'll be fine. Trust me."

"Famous last words," she grumbled.

"Stop complaining. I'm getting in the zone."

Mona tutted beside him. He eased the car to a halt behind the target's and got out of the vehicle.

The man lowered his window and frowned, "Is there a problem?"

"Yes, sir. I'm just being a good citizen, but your bumper is lopsided. I thought I'd let you know in case it dropped off and caused any damage to anyone following you."

"What? I've only just got it back from the garage." He opened the car door.

Warren took a step back. The target attempted to get out of the vehicle, but Warren leapt forward and bashed the door against his legs. The man cried out.

"What the hell is going on here?"

Warren produced a set of zip ties and ordered, "Sit there and shut up. Put your hands on the steering wheel."

The man hesitated for a moment or two and then finally relented. Warren slipped the ties on each of the target's wrists and around the steering wheel then beckoned Mona to join him. At first, she was reluctant. He marched back to the car. "Don't do this, not now. We need to act quickly. Get the can."

"You're making a mistake. I told you, it's far too open."

"Get a grip, woman."

She exited the vehicle and removed a petrol can from the back seat. She handed it to Warren, and he marched back to the target's car and proceeded to pour the contents of the can over the roof and bonnet of the BMW.

The target looked horrified and shouted, "What are you doing? You can't do that? Are you insane?"

Warren grinned. "Possibly." He emptied the remains of the can and then threw it back to Mona, who returned it to the back seat once more.

"Don't do this. Let's discuss this like adults before you do something you're likely to regret."

"I doubt it. You're on the kill list. You were supposed to be the last one, but the boss rang and, well, you got elevated to the top position."

"What are you talking about? What *kill list*? Who are you?"

"Question after bloody question, don't you ever stop with the cross-examining?"

"No, never. I have an enquiring mind. I demand to know what your intentions are."

"I haven't got time to stand around here chatting all day. I've got places to go and people to see." He closed the driver's door to block out the man's incessant talking and eventual screams. Then he removed a box of matches from his jacket pocket and stood in front of the car. He saw the man shouting, shaking his head and panicking to get his hands out of the ties restraining him.

"Say goodbye, big man." He struck several matches at once and aimed them at the car. A couple of them blew out in the evening breeze. He lit a couple more and threw them onto the roof.

The target's expression was one of horror. He shouted for Warren to help him. Warren ensured the car was engulfed in the flames then raced back to his own vehicle and pulled away.

"Jesus, that poor man," Mona mumbled.

"Don't go feeling sorry for the fucker."

"He was only doing his job, of course I'm going to feel sorry for him. I hate this."

"You'd better get used to it, this is just the beginning. We've got another one to kill off tonight. Then another two every night until the list has been completed."

"Jesus, that's a lot of pressure on us. I'm not sure I'm going to be able to cope."

"You will. We have to."

"And what happens if they ask you to do extra hours at work, what then?"

"Then you'll have to take over." He turned and grinned broadly.

"You can go fuck yourself, I'm not doing it."

"We'll see. We've got a few hours' grace before we kill the next one. Why don't we go and have something to eat?"

Mona shook her head and sank into her seat. Warren made a U-turn in the road and passed the blazing car seconds later. It exploded when they were around fifty feet away. Then they drove back into town.

"Bye-bye, Mr Third Victim."

"You're sick. I can't believe you're frigging enjoying this."

6

Sara was tucked up on the sofa, having a cuddle with Mark and Misty when she received the call. Mark groaned, which was unlike him.

"Sorry, love. I'll take it in the kitchen." She leapt out of her seat and left the room. "DI Ramsey."

"Ever so sorry to disturb you, ma'am. It's control here. I thought you'd want to hear this."

"What's *this*?"

"We've been informed a man has perished in a blaze on the A465 out near Belmont."

"And? Can't someone else attend for a change? I worked a fifteen-hour shift yesterday." She rolled her eyes and sighed, aware that complaining about the situation wouldn't matter a damn jot. "Sorry, ignore me. I'm grouchy today. Perished in a blaze… care to enlighten me as to how that happened?"

"He was in his car and it went up in flames."

"And what exactly am I supposed to do about that?"

"The pathologist suggested I should give you a call because she's regarding it as a suspicious death."

"I take it she's at the scene?"

"Yes, that's right, ma'am."

"All right. I'll put my shoes on and get over there. No rest for the wicked, is there?"

"I feel for you. Sorry, ma'am."

"Don't be. I'll give the pathologist a call en route."

"As you wish, ma'am. Thank you."

Sara ended the call and walked back into the lounge. Mark stared up at her and closed his eyes. "Don't tell me you've got to go out again!"

"I'm sorry, Mark. There's no one else available."

"That's convenient."

"Please, love, don't be like this. We're understaffed at the best of times. This is a one-off, I promise."

His eyes shot open. "How can it be a one-off when you worked a fifteen-hour shift yesterday?"

"I'm sorry, you're right. It was a stupid thing for me to say. I'm going to have to fly."

"Is Carla going to attend as well?"

"I'm not sure. I forgot to check with control. I can handle it on my own." She took a step towards him and hugged him. He was rigid in her arms. Most unusual for him. He was generally understanding about her job, not tonight, apparently.

"I won't wait up."

"I'm sorry, Mark." It was the last thing she said to him before she left the house. She drove to the location with her brain working over-time. *Is my marriage on the rocks? It can't be, we're so happy. But why did he turn on me like that? And on top of what's happening to Mum, too. I won't be able to cope if Mark turns on me. How many police officers' marriages go to pot? I don't want to be a statistic.*

Lorraine's red hair stuck out in the makeshift lights that had been erected at the scene. The fire engine was just leaving the lay-by when she pulled up. Lorraine came to meet her, wearing an apologetic smile. "Sorry, matey. I tried not to get you involved, but the woman on control said everyone else was tied up for the evening."

"It's fine. What have we got?"

"The victim perished in the blaze. I know the car's a mess, but it seems a pretty new one to me. One of the firemen said the model had only been out since last year. There's no reason for it to go up in smoke."

Sara glanced at the car. "Silly question, have you run the plate? Or did anyone else think to do it?" She noticed at least four uniformed officers and two patrol cars in the vicinity.

"I haven't, not sure if your mob have or not."

"I'll be back in a tick." She stormed across to where the four officers were standing around chatting. "Sorry to interrupt your important meeting, gents, has anyone bothered to run the plates through the system?"

"Umm... I was just in the process of doing that, ma'am."

"You were? Hard to believe when all I see is four coppers wasting time, chatting. Let's get busy, gents, before I get in touch with the desk sergeant, make him aware of what's going on here."

Three of the men drifted off, and the fourth man radioed the station to give them the plate number. The information came back quickly.

"Wow. Okay, thanks. I'll pass it on to the SIO."

"What did they say?" Sara asked, intrigued by the man's surprised expression.

"The car belongs to a Miles Chaddock."

Sara frowned. "I know that name, where do I know it from?"

"He's the high-profile solicitor, Miles Chaddock," the officer replied with a raised eyebrow.

"Bugger. Not what I expected to hear. I'm going to need his address. Can you get that for me while I inform the pathologist?"

"Leave it with me, ma'am."

Sara was still shaking her head by the time she reached Lorraine who was collecting something from the back of her van.

"Everything all right?" Lorraine asked. "You seem puzzled."

"I am. I've just discovered who the car belongs to."

"And? I'm dying of suspense here."

"A local prosecuting solicitor."

"Shit! What the fuck?"

"My thoughts exactly. Was this intentional?"

"I won't know until I examine the vehicle thoroughly. Do you want to throw a suit on and take a closer look with me?"

"Not particularly, but I will."

Lorraine smiled. "Tough day for you, eh?"

"It's getting tougher by the minute. Mark fell out with me before I left."

"What? You two are rock solid. How come?"

"He wasn't too happy about me attending the call-out. I can't blame him but what else am I supposed to do when we're short-staffed and up against it?"

"I can understand where you're both coming from. You were out last night as well, after putting in a full day at work. You must be knackered, Sara. I suppose he's guilty of looking out for you. Give him a break."

"I guess. Hey, you're out and about, too. You can't have had much rest in between jobs either."

"There's a significant difference between you and me. I'm an old spinster with nothing better to do, and you're a fit young married woman with a hot husband waiting at home for you."

"If you say so." Sara slipped into the suit Lorraine had supplied.

"Anyway, I'm hopeless at handing out relationship advice. So let's crack on."

"Is it safe? Looks like it's still smouldering a touch to me."

"It'll soon die down. The brigade wouldn't have left if there was any chance of the fire starting up again."

"I'll take your word for that."

They approached the car, and one of the SOCO techs opened the driver's door. Sara flinched. She hated witnessing the charred remains of victims, always had done.

"I detest the smell of burning flesh," she grumbled, placing a gloved hand over her mouth and nose.

"I don't think anyone likes it, especially if they've recently had a barbecue." Lorraine laughed, chipping through the sombre atmosphere.

"Gross. Did you have to say that?"

"What? It's the truth. Anyway, stand back and let me have a good root around in here."

Sara peered through the rear window. There was something lying on the back seat. She opened the door. "His briefcase is in here. Or should I say, what's left of it."

"Okay, we'll put it in an evidence bag. Wait, what's this?" Lorraine bent down and peered into the footwell by the pedals.

"What's that?"

Lorraine held up what appeared to be a piece of plastic.

"Looks like one of those ties you put around a tree to hold it in place, doesn't it?" Sara suggested.

"It does. A zip tie." Lorraine examined the victim's hands. "One of his arms is on the steering wheel and his other is beside him."

"Meaning?"

"I don't know. Maybe he was tied to the steering wheel, I'll have to examine his wrists for any signs of restraint."

Sara nodded, her mind catching up with Lorraine's proposal. "You reckon the flames cut through the plastic, one side quicker than the other perhaps? Can you see anything around the arm on the steering wheel?"

"Not yet. Wait, yes, it's adjoined to the steering wheel still. Jesus, you know what this means, don't you?"

"He was murdered," Sara took a punt.

"Correct. Bloody hell."

Sara took a step back and assessed how busy the road was. Relatively quiet, for now.

"What are you thinking?" Lorraine asked.

"He's parked in a lay-by, why?"

"Are you thinking he had arranged to meet someone here?"

Sara shrugged. "Possibly." She backed away and called over to the uniformed officer who was on the radio to the station, "Any luck with his address yet?"

The officer jotted down something in his notebook and scurried over to her. "Sorry it took so long, there was a slight glitch with the system, they had to reboot the computer." He tore off the sheet of paper and gave it to Sara.

"It doesn't matter. Hmm… he lives just up the road in Belmont. Okay, thanks for this. Get the area cordoned off. I don't think it's going to take four of you to do that. Send two officers on their way."

"Will do, ma'am." He walked away.

"What are you thinking now?" Lorraine whispered in her ear.

"Shit, you bloody nearly made my heart stop, creeping up on me like that."

"Sorry. I thought you heard me behind you."

"Nope. I was lost in thought."

"No shit, Sherlock!"

"Give me a break. Hear me out. What if he was on his way home from the office and he discovered he was being followed? Maybe he pulled in to see if the car following him drove past."

"Possibly. What if he stopped to take a call and a car drew up behind him?"

"And someone took an instant dislike to him and decided to torch the car with him inside it?"

Lorraine's mouth twisted. "All right, when you put it like that, it does sound ludicrous, I must admit."

"I think I'll go with my scenario. That he was most likely followed here, maybe the person in the second car intimated there was something wrong with the solicitor's vehicle."

"But why? Why out here?"

"He might have been working late at the office. This is his route home. Maybe he wasn't followed at all, maybe the killer was already parked in the lay-by and flagged him down as he passed, asking him to assist them."

"Both viable options in my opinion. You should be a detective." Lorraine's wise remark gained her a slap on the arm from Sara.

"I'm trying to be serious here, if you don't mind."

"My apologies. This place was probably chosen on purpose, we're in the middle of nowhere, no sign of any cameras around."

"You read my mind. Okay, I'm going to leave you to it and seek out his next of kin, unless you want to swap duties for the next couple of hours?"

"Sure thing. Let me jot down what will be expected of you. Number one, take skin samples of the charred remains."

Sara grimaced. "Yeah, okay, stop right there. I've heard enough already."

"I thought you'd soon change your mind."

"I'll crack on and drop back after I've spoken to the family, if you're still here."

"I'll probably still be here at midnight. This type of examination can be lengthy compared to the normal victims I usually have to deal with."

"I'll wish you luck and bid you farewell in that case."

"Ditto. See you later."

Sara hopped back in her car and left the scene. She drove a few hundred yards and then took a sharp right. Another hundred yards or so and a large mansion set back from the road came into view. She checked the address against what was written down to find it matched. *I suppose I should have expected this, given his job.*

Sara entered the long driveway, and the tyres crunched over the deep gravel. It was lit up with coloured spotlights on either side. The house itself was grand in stature with Georgian windows and a columned stone porch at the top of three wide steps. She steadied her racing heart with a few large breaths, exited the vehicle and jogged up the steps. The bell was attached to a long metal handle. While she waited for the door to open, the clear night sky caught her eye. The glittering stars were in abundance this evening.

"Hello, can I help you?"

The woman's voice cut through Sara's mesmerised state. "Sorry, yes. I'm DI Sara Ramsey. Would it be okay if I came in to speak with you, Mrs Chaddock?" Sara showed the woman her warrant card.

The woman, dressed in a smart cream suit edged with pearl buttons, frowned. "What's the meaning of this visit, and at this late hour?"

"Sorry to intrude. It would be better if we spoke inside."

"Very well. Come in. My husband is due home soon."

Sara entered the house, and the woman peered up the driveway, obviously on the lookout for her husband.

She closed the door and folded her arms as she faced Sara. "So, what's all this about?"

"Mummy, is that Daddy? I want to show him my new tutu."

"No, darling. He won't be long. Stay upstairs until he comes home, that way you'll give him the biggest surprise ever."

"Okay." Heavy footsteps sounded on the landing above.

"How old is she?" Sara enquired.

"Five, going on twenty-eight. She's the apple of my husband's eye. They're inseparable when he's at home." She anxiously glanced at her watch and then gasped. "Oh no, my mind was elsewhere at the time you first spoke to me. Tell me, why are you here? Has something happened to him?"

Sara's gaze drifted to the stairs, and she lowered her voice, "Perhaps we should talk about this somewhere less open."

Mrs Chaddock slapped a hand to her chest and nodded. "Come through to the lounge." Two sets of heels clicked on the marble floor until the lush oatmeal-coloured carpet in the main living room deadened the noise. Mrs Chaddock took a seat by the roaring open fire ablaze in the inglenook fireplace and invited Sara to sit on the two-seater Chesterfield sofa close to her. "Please, tell me what's happened. Is my husband coming home?"

Sara inhaled a large breath and shook her head. "I'm so sorry, but no. Your husband lost his life this evening when his car burst into flames."

"What? Are you sure it was him? How do you know it was him?" The words tumbled out of the woman's mouth so quickly that they seemed to be all merged together.

"The pathologist will need to perform a post-mortem. Until then, we won't be able to fully verify that it was your husband in the car. Is there any reason not to think he'd be driving the vehicle this evening?"

The stunned woman shook her head. "No."

"Was your husband due home around this time?"

"Yes. He's later than usual this evening. Oh God, I can't believe I'm hearing this. How will the children cope without him? And me for that matter."

"I'm so sorry for your loss. Are you up to answering a few questions?"

She sniffled. "Would you be?"

"I understand. Maybe we should leave things there for now and I'll call back to see you in the morning."

Mrs Chaddock bowed her head, and the tears fell into her lap. She dabbed her eyes with the hankie. "No, ignore me. I apologise for snapping at you. You being here is such a shock. It's our anniversary, we had plans to go out for a late dinner this evening. The babysitter is due in twenty minutes, I suppose I won't be needing her services now." More tears tumbled onto her beautifully made-up face. "What is wrong with me? I'm not the crying type. But losing the love of your life at his age, I simply can't get my head around what you've told me. How did it happen? His car was relatively new, there was no reason for it to just burst into flames, not unless there was some kind of manufacturing fault. If that's the case, I'll be suing their arses off. Robbing me of my wonderful husband like this."

"I don't believe that's the case. I've just left the scene, it happened in a lay-by on the main road, not far from here."

"In a lay-by? Did he stop to answer a call? If he did, that would be a first for him. I've told him a million times to pull over to answer his hands-free, but he always refused to do it."

"At the scene, the pathologist and I assessed your husband's body and found some form of plastic close to him."

"Sorry? What sort of plastic are you talking about?"

"As in a plastic tie," Sara explained.

"I'm not with you. As far as I know my husband didn't possess any ties of that kind, let alone carry them in the car."

"What we believe is that your husband was possibly tied to the steering wheel."

Mrs Chaddock tilted her head and frowned. "I don't understand, what am I missing here? You're going to have to spell it out for me, Inspector, because at the moment, my head is in a spin, trying to figure this out."

"It is our belief that your husband may have been tied to the steering wheel before the car was intentionally set on fire."

The woman stared at her for a long time, shaking her head in disbelief. "No, this can't be right. What are you saying? That you think someone killed my husband?"

Sara nodded. "Yes."

Mrs Chaddock broke down and cried. Just then the doorbell rang. "Oh no, that'll be the babysitter. Please, will you send her away? Tell her we won't be needing her this evening after all."

"Of course. I'll be right back." Sara left the room and rushed to the front door. A teenage girl seemed surprised to see Sara open it.

"Who are you? Where's Mrs Chaddock?"

"Are you the babysitter?"

"Yes. Who are you?" the teenager screeched.

"I'm the police. The family have had some upsetting news. Mrs Chaddock asked me to tell you that she won't be needing your services this evening."

"What news? Are the children okay?" The girl stood on her tiptoes and peered over Sara's shoulder.

"Yes, they're fine. I'm sure Mrs Chaddock will be in touch with you soon. Goodbye." Sara closed the door in the girl's astonished face and returned to the lounge to find that Mrs Chaddock had poured herself a large brandy or whisky.

"Was she all right about not coming in?"

"She was fine. A little shocked because I refused to go into detail as to why you wouldn't be needing her. Are you okay?"

"I know the feeling. I feel shocked and numb by what you revealed earlier. Who would do such a thing to Miles? I know he wasn't the best person to get on with, but he didn't deserve to go out like this."

"I take it your husband could be a handful at times?"

"Yes, I suppose it went with the job. He was a solicitor, I'm not sure if you knew that or not?"

"I was aware. I have to ask if he's had any form of threat made against him recently."

"Threat? No, well, not that I'm aware of. I have to tell you that he was a very secretive man, made a point of keeping his work life separate from his home life. He adored the children, spent as much time as he could interacting with them at the weekends and during the holidays. He was keen to make up for the childhood he never had with his own father. He was a judge and always put his work first, never once found the time to spend with Miles. They went on holiday to Brighton once. He told me his father sat at the desk in the hotel room, going over his notes, the whole time they were away. His mother was livid, caused a blazing row, which ended with the family cutting their holiday short and returning home. His father went back to work immediately upon his return." She took a sip from her glass and shuddered as the liquid burnt her throat on the way down. "Miles wasn't an easy man to live with by any means, but he would never have treated us like his father treated him back in the day."

"He tried to find a good balance between work and home," Sara added.

"Yes. He was a very stern man towards adults, but the children appeared to melt his heart as soon as he walked through the front door."

"Did he ever have any problems with the clients he worked with?"

"Always. Take your pick if you're asking me if he fell out with his clients. He did that on a regular basis."

"Oh dear. Do you think a client might be behind his death?"

She shrugged. "You tell me, you're the detective. Look, I didn't really get involved in his business. If you want to know the ins and outs of what went on at the office, you're asking the wrong person. My advice would be to speak with either his personal assistant or his partners at the firm. I refused to get involved, the children and their upbringing continued to be my priority, that was our arrangement.

Once the children were at boarding school then I would return to my work of running an advertising agency. My partner has agreed to run it for me for the last seven years, since Kent was born."

"I see. Perhaps you can tell me if your husband has received any strange phone calls in the evenings while he's been at home with you?"

"No, nothing that I can think of. I'm sorry I'm no help, it's just the setup we had. Home time was family time and work matters remained in the car outside. It worked out well for us. The children had a stable upbringing, having our full attention most of the time."

"I understand. What about any strangers, either coming to the house or approaching your husband? Did he give you any indication something like that might have taken place?"

"No. If it did, he kept it from me."

"Did he mention if someone had followed him lately?"

"Nothing that I can think of. Honestly, if I could recall anything out of the ordinary happening in the last few weeks or so, I would tell you. Damn, how the hell am I going to tell the children that they will never see their father again?"

"That's a difficult problem for any mother to deal with, my heart goes out to you."

Her gaze fixed on Sara. "Inspector, I don't need your sympathy, what I need is for you to find the person who has torn my family apart this evening. Are you capable of doing that?"

"I have every confidence my team and I will do just that, given time. We're in the middle of investigating two other crimes at the moment."

"Whoa! Wait just a second, so what you're telling me is that you won't be prioritising my husband's case, is that correct?"

"No, that's not what I was saying at all. I'm trying to reassure you that I have an experienced team, we'll take on your husband's case as well, and you have my assurance that we will do our utmost to find the culprit, swiftly."

"Thank goodness."

"Is there anything else you can tell me?"

"Such as? Forgive me if you think I'm being obstructive with the information I have given you this evening, you see, I've never found myself in such an untenable situation before."

"I completely understand. What about family members, any problems there? Did your husband have any relatives in the area?"

"No, none at all. We moved from Bath over fifteen years ago. He has a brother who is a barrister in that area. I have a sister who owns a beauty spa, also in Bath. Neither of them has ever had any form of trouble land on their doorstep, not as far as I'm aware anyway."

"Would it be possible to have their names and addresses before I leave?"

"I'll get them now." She left her seat and fetched her handbag from the small desk on the other side of the room, alongside the patio doors which led out to a lit seating area of the garden. Sara saw her scroll through her phone and jot down the details Sara needed. Her gaze drifted around the room and picked up on all the family photos displayed on some of the surfaces. Miles Chaddock had been a very handsome man in his early forties, if the photos were anything to go by.

Mrs Chaddock returned and handed Sara two sheets of paper. "My sister's and Miles' brother's details."

"Thank you, you're very kind. Are you going to be all right, here on your own, I mean?"

"Except I'm not alone, I have the children to deal with. It's almost their bedtime, they're bound to ask me where their father is, he's usually the one who settles them down every night. They'll miss that interaction the most, I think." She fell silent for a few moments as more tears surfaced. "I'm sorry. Will I ever stop crying?"

"In time. It took me quite a few months to get over the death of my husband."

Mrs Chaddock swiftly glanced up at Sara. "Your husband died?"

"Murdered by a gang in Liverpool. He died in my arms."

"Goodness me. I'm so sorry for your loss. Can I ask if you have children?"

"No. I've never had them. I can't possibly imagine how difficult the next few weeks are going to be for you, but I'll leave you my card with the invitation to ring me if you ever need to chat. This initial period can be a lonely one for a widow."

"Thank you. It'll be good to know I can count on you for support, should I need it."

Sara took a card from her pocket and left her seat. She handed it to Mrs Chaddock and turned to leave the room. The woman showed her to the door just as a little boy and girl came tearing down the grand sweeping staircase.

"Mummy, where's our daddy?" the little girl asked, disappointment edging her tone.

"He'll be home shortly, dears. Now go back upstairs and clean your teeth."

The children glanced at each other and then raced up the stairs, giggling.

"The innocence of children," Mrs Chaddock whispered.

Sara placed a hand on top of hers and smiled. "I hope it goes well, telling them. We have counsellors available, should you need them."

"Thank you. I'll see how I go. I might take you up on that offer if things don't go as expected. Do your very best for us, Inspector."

"You have my word. My condolences once again."

She smiled, and her eyes glistened. Sara left, feeling her words sounded inadequate, even to her own ears. She drove back to the crime scene suddenly exhausted by the substantial events the day had thrown at her.

"Something tells me your visit didn't go too well," Lorraine croaked. She dipped into the driver's side of her van and downed half a can of Diet Coke. "Damn fumes are still lingering, playing havoc with my throat."

"Sorry to hear that, it must be a nightmare to contend with. The visit went as well as could be expected, I suppose. I think it's the day catching up on me."

"Sara, go home. You shouldn't still be out here, not after dealing with all your personal crap, love."

"I think you're right. How are things going here?"

Lorraine peered over her shoulder at the car. "They're going, that's about all I can tell you right now."

Sara's mobile rang. She answered it, trying to sound as bright as a button. "DI Ramsey."

"Hello, ma'am, it's the control room here."

"I'm listening. I have a feeling I'm not going to like what you're about to say."

"Sorry, I think your instincts are correct, ma'am. We've had a call about yet another murder. I was wondering if you could attend."

"I'm at the crime scene that was reported earlier, actually, I'm with the pathologist. I'm going to put you on speaker so she can listen in. Where and who?"

"In the centre of Hereford, close to the Barbells Gym, do you know it?"

"Not personally. I've never set foot in one of those places. And the *who*?"

"A young man."

"Damn. Okay, and there are definitely no other units available to take on the case?"

"Sorry, I did try, knowing that you've been at it since first thing this morning, but we have the huge people trafficking and the other large drug cases taking precedence for most of the inspectors at present."

"Whittling it down, that leaves me and my team to pick up the slack. Fair enough, I can't stamp my feet and argue. I take it the area has been cordoned off by uniform?"

"Yes, ma'am. That side of things has been taken care of. I was about to contact the pathologist next."

"No need. Lorraine has heard everything. She's doing the best she can at this location but will probably be delayed getting to the next scene. Secure the area, she'll be there as soon as humanly possible."

"Very well. Thank you, ma'am."

Sara ended the call. Lorraine seemed a bit miffed. "You all right?"

"Not in the slightest. What gives with all these murders? That's four separate cases we're dealing with this week alone."

"Yeah, don't remind me. So much bloody anger in this world, it's really ticking me off now. Since lockdown occurred, it appears to have got so much worse."

Lorraine nodded. "I agree. Peoples' tolerance levels are at a bare minimum. I'm sorry but I'm going to be a good few hours here."

"Why should you apologise? It's not like you're sat at home putting your feet up in front of an exceptional film, is it?"

"Don't even go there. I can't remember when I had any time off to do something like that."

Sara wagged her finger. "What have I told you about employing someone else to ease the burden always falling on your shoulders?"

"I've tried, believe me."

Sara shook her head. "Try harder. You need to get some form of life back, Lorraine."

Her pathologist friend raised an eyebrow and folded her arms. "Says you. Out here at all hours when you should be curled up on the sofa with that stud of a husband of yours."

"I know. It's a case of do as I say and not as I do. Seriously, if you don't get some time off soon, you're going to collapse in a heap, and then where would we all be?"

"All right. Nagging session over. Haven't you got a crime scene to attend?"

"I can take a hint. Do you know where the gym is?"

"I think so. I'll check with one of my team before I head over there."

"Right." Sara blew out an exasperated breath. "I suppose I'll see you later."

"My suggestion would be for you to wait in the car, maybe grab a quick nap. I sense we're both in for a long night."

"A nap? Are you kidding me?"

Lorraine grinned. "Wishful thinking, right? Laters."

Sara hopped in her car and drove into town. En route, she took a while to pluck up the courage to call home. "Hi, Mark. Umm… sorry to have to tell you that I'm going to be a while yet."

"Oh, may I ask why?" His tone was clipped, which tore at Sara's heart. He'd never spoken to her like that before.

I suppose there's a first time for everything.

For some reason, she felt the need to stretch the truth a little. "I was just on my way home when control rang me and informed me that yet another body had been found. So I need to attend, see what we're dealing with."

"And you're the only police officer on duty, in the whole of Hereford, is that what you're telling me?"

"No, I mean, yes. There are plenty of uniformed officers on duty, but all the other inspectors are indisposed this evening. They've got their hands full with two major investigations."

Mark fell quiet. She was beginning to wonder if he'd hung up on her.

"Mark, are you still there?"

"I'm here. What do you want me to say, Sara? That it's fine you working all these hours?"

"I'm not expecting you to say anything, all I'm asking is for a little understanding. I know things are tough right now. I've never been a copper who worked nine to five, you're aware of that."

He blew out a breath. "I know that. Just ignore me, I'm sitting here with Misty, feeling sorry for myself. I know I'm being a hypocrite, I'm aware I work exceedingly long hours myself more often than not. I suppose I was hoping we could spend some time together while the surgery is going through a lull right now."

"I get that and I'm truly sorry. I'll make it up to you, I promise." She indicated and pulled up alongside one of the patrol cars parked at the crime scene. "I've got to go now. Are we all right? I'd hate to think that my job is going to damage our relationship. If that's the case then maybe I should reconsider my career, especially after what Mum is going through."

"Damn, now you're making me feel bad about being cranky. We're fine, Sara. I'm the one being selfish, not you. You warned me right at the beginning what it might be like. Want me to check in with your father, see how your mum is tonight?"

Tears welled up. His anger had dissipated, and he'd instantly flipped back to being the kind and compassionate man she'd married. "If you wouldn't mind. I've been constantly thinking about her during the day."

"I know. Again, that's why I feel so selfish for having a go at you. You're doing your best when the odds are stacked against you. I'll send them your love. Stay safe, Sara, I love you."

"I love you, too. Don't worry about me. I'm sure things will settle down soon enough. Don't wait up, it could be a late one. What am I saying? It will be a late one, it already is."

"I'll have a snuggle with Misty, it'll make everything all right again."

"That's the ticket. I'll ring you later."

"Speak soon. We're with you in spirit."

She ended the call and exited the vehicle. After togging up in a protective suit, she signed the Crime Scene Log and dipped under the cordon. Pulling on a pair of gloves, she approached the victim. He was dressed in jogging pants and a grey hooded sweatshirt which was covered in blood. She winced and inched a little closer to discover his throat had been cut. He hadn't stood a chance. Sara glanced around and approached one of the uniformed officers. "Who found him and called it in?"

"The manager of the gym. He's inside."

"Thanks, do you know his name?"

"Terry Mullins. I said someone would be in to interview him shortly."

"I'll see him now. Have you got a clean sheet in the car? Something we can use to cover the body until the pathologist arrives?" Sara mentally kicked herself for not thinking to ask Lorraine for one back at the other crime scene.

"I'll see what we can scrabble together between us."

"It needs to be clean, if not, it would be better to leave the body exposed rather than cause any cross-contamination."

"I understand. Leave it with me."

She stripped off her suit and deposited it in a black sack then walked the length of the alley to the gym at the rear and entered the main entrance. There were a couple of members of staff, lingering in the reception area. Sara produced her warrant card. "I'm DI Ramsey, I'd like a word with the manager, Terry Mullins, is it?"

"Yes, that's right. He's in his office. I'll just ask if he has time to see you," the blonde with the petite but muscle-bound figure replied. She left the area and returned with a man in his thirties who was sporting a small beard.

"I'm Terry Mullins. Would you rather do this in my office?"

"Thanks. I'm DI Ramsey. If you wouldn't mind."

He led the way to a small office a few feet down a short corridor and gestured for her to take a seat. The office had a glass wall at the rear which overlooked the main area of the gym. "I see you have a bird's eye view."

"Yes. I while away the hours in here, watching over the staff and ensuring they are instructing their clients correctly at all times."

"A form of spying on your staff then?"

"I wouldn't necessarily say that. It's important my staff treat the customers well. The last thing I want is for any of them to have an injury. Can you imagine the costs involved in a negligence claim?"

"I'm with you. I suppose keeping fit can be a risky business and carry a hefty insurance package."

"You're not kidding. You don't want to know how much it costs to run a place like this. Anyway, you've not come to discuss my woes, have you?"

Sara liked the manager, he had an affable manner and a cute smile. "Sadly not. I take it you found the body, is that right?"

"Yes. Actually, I saw the incident on the CCTV footage, or some of it."

"What? Can you show me?"

"Sure. We'll need to go next door."

They nipped into the next room. He pulled up two chairs and positioned them in front of the monitor. He pressed Play, and the scene started.

"I take it the victim had been at the gym, judging by the clothes he was wearing."

"That's right. José was a regular here, came every other day to maintain his fitness levels, as advised. A lot of good it did him in the end."

"Such a shame. How were you aware of the attack?" Sara peered at the screen; it was dark in the alley. She had noticed it was lit at the other end by a flickering streetlight.

"I happened to be in here, collecting some paper for the copying machine. I walked past the monitor and saw the skirmish. I ran out there, took a couple of the fitness instructors with me, but by the time we reached him it was too late. The poor bugger's throat was slit from ear to ear. I must tell you, the pile of vomit in the corner was from Ken, he's a bit of a wuss. He started retching, and I had enough sense to pull him away from the scene."

"Excellent work. Thanks for letting me know. So this happened what? Around thirty minutes ago?"

"Yes, around nine-thirty. José usually had a routine. He came here at seven-fifteen and generally worked out until nine-fifteen. After that, he collected his bag from the locker room and left straight away. He's not one to hang around to have a shower, he'd rather get home to the missus. Blast, Sonia is going to be mortified. They only got wed last summer, and she's expecting their first child."

Sara heaved out an exasperated breath. "Jesus, that's tough. I'll need his address before I leave. You'll have that on file, won't you?"

"I can sort it out for you after you've viewed the footage. This is the part you'll find interesting, coming up now."

Sara's eyes were glued to the screen. She had to move in close to see exactly what was going on. "Damn council needs to get the streetlights sorted out around here," she complained.

"Can you have a word? I'm sick to death of writing to them, telling them how dangerous it is for our female customers to leave the gym at night."

"I'll get onto them first thing, don't worry. Shame it takes a tragedy such as this to get things sorted."

"This is it. José was close to the end of the alley, the car park is just around the corner. I'm presuming that's where he parked every time he came here."

Sara jumped when two figures sprang from nowhere. "Jesus, well... they scared the crap out of me."

"Yeah, I had the same reaction. I have to confess, it took me a few seconds to realise what was happening and to rally the troops to get out there. It was hopeless, though. He was already dead."

Sara nodded and kept her gaze on the screen, watching the vicious attack and cringing each time the victim received a blow from one of his two attackers. "Bastards," she mumbled.

"I have to agree with you. Cowards as well, to attack him where they know the lights are dodgy."

Sara nodded but thought more about his statement. *Had the attack taken place intentionally in this area? Knowing the lighting was faulty and their identities would be disguised?*

The attack lasted around thirty seconds before the larger of the two assailants withdrew a large knife and slit the man's throat. He hit the ground quickly, gasping for breath. Sara took that to mean the assailant knew exactly how deep to make the cut. *We could be looking at a professional kill here.*

Once the attack was over and the assailants had legged it, Sara asked, "Can I trouble you for a copy?"

"Sure. I'll do it now."

She watched Terry's shaking hands remove a disc from its case. "Are you all right?"

He smiled and nodded. "A little shaken up still, but at least I'm alive, unlike José."

She took the disc from his hand. "Tell me what to do with the disc."

"Thanks. I feel such a fool."

"It shows you care. Don't put yourself down."

"Insert it in there. It would probably take me a few attempts to get it in the tiny slit."

Sara did as instructed and stood back while he hit a few buttons, rewound the original disc to where José left the gym and pressed the Record button.

She watched the attack in more detail the second time, focussing on the assailants to see if anything jumped out at her. It didn't. It was as if they knew where the camera was and did everything they could to ensure they avoided it. With the transfer complete, Terry handed her the disc case and led the way back to his office.

Seated at his desk, he brought his computer to life and searched the database for what he needed. Picking up a pen, he scribbled something down and handed it to Sara. "José's address for you."

"Did you know him very well?"

"Sort of. We had a couple of chats about fitness a few times over the years. He joined the gym maybe three years ago. He was a little overweight and wanted to regain the fitness levels he used to have in his teens. He was a keen athlete back then but stopped when he started going out with Sonia. It was she who had encouraged him to join the gym in the first place."

"Did he ever speak about personal things?"

"Such as?"

"I don't know... ever hint that he was in some kind of trouble, perhaps?"

"No, nothing like that at all." He pointed as he contemplated his answer further. "There was something a couple of months ago. He missed a few sessions. I asked him if everything was all right. He told me he'd been on jury duty and was mentally exhausted by the time he got home every night. It went on a few weeks, I think. He enjoyed it, it just took a lot out of him, so he decided something had to give. He got back on track the week after the trial had ended."

"I see. So he was definitely committed to his regime."

"Absolutely. I'll miss him around here. He had a great sense of humour."

"José? Was he British?"

"Yes, although I think he told me his parents were from Portugal.

They returned a few years ago, but he refused to go with them. He and Sonia had recently started dating, and it became serious pretty quickly, I believe."

"Ah, the love of a woman," Sara said, smiling. It slipped when she realised what her next task was going to be. "Okay, it's late now, would it be all right if I sent a uniformed officer to see you tomorrow, to take down your statement?"

"That'd be great. I was hoping you wouldn't be expecting one tonight. We close at ten, and then I have to spend an hour or so cashing up and making sure everything is locked up, that sort of thing."

"I understand. I'll be off now. Thank you for trying to help the victim and for giving me a copy of the footage. I'm sure it will make all the difference to our investigation. For a start, we now know there were two assailants and not just the one."

"I hope it helps capture them. The bastards need to be locked up for good after taking José's life."

"I'm not about to disagree with you. We're going to give it our best shot. You've given us the heads up an investigation needs from the word go."

"Glad to hear it."

He saw Sara to the main entrance and shook her hand. She made her way back to the crime scene. The uniformed officers on site had done their best to secure the scene with the appropriate amount of tape and managed to cover the body with a new white sheet.

"How did you get on?" the officer who had supplied her with the manager's name enquired.

"As well as could be expected, I suppose. Are you lot okay here? I'm not ducking out, I promise. I'd like to visit the wife before it gets any later. She'll be anticipating his arrival."

"We can hang around, no problem, ma'am. Is there anything we can do while we're here?"

"Maybe a couple of you can watch over the victim while the others go house-to-house. See if anyone either heard or saw anything before or after the attack. Maybe someone spotted the assailants escaping and can tell us in which direction they went and what vehicle they were driving. I've been given a copy of the CCTV footage showing the attack. They didn't hang around; seemed like the vic was targeted intentionally."

"We'll do that. So there were two attackers. Could you make out what gender they were?"

"No, both were wearing hoods. Do your best for me. The pathologist should be here within a couple of hours."

"Don't worry. Leave it with us, ma'am."

"I'm going to have to." Sara smiled and went back to her car. She glanced at the sheet of paper and entered the postcode into the satnav.

Fifteen minutes later, she parked outside a cute, gardenless, semi-detached house on a small estate. There was a light on in the front room. She left the car, knocked on the front door and waited for José's wife to open it.

A heavily pregnant woman with black hair tied up in a bun wrenched the door open. She gasped, clearly expecting to find her late husband standing there. "Oh. Who are you?" She took a step forward and searched the road up and down. "I thought you were my husband. He's late, you see."

Sara flashed her ID. "Mrs Hickman, I'm DI Sara Ramsey. Would it be all right if I came in and spoke to you for a moment?"

"To me? What about?"

Sara stared at her and smiled sympathetically. It didn't take Mrs Hickman long to cotton on. She staggered and hit the wall as her legs gave way. Despite her weariness, Sara leapt forward and saved Sonia from dropping to the floor. She closed the front door with her foot and helped the woman into the first room off the hallway. The lounge was filled with wedding photos; there was a huge canvas of the couple on the far wall. Sara pushed down the bile burning her throat. She settled the woman onto the sofa and sat next to her.

"What's happened to him? Please tell me he's still alive."

"I'm sorry. I'm afraid your husband died at the scene."

Sonia Hickman screamed and then wailed. "No. No. No. He can't be dead." She cradled her bump and then ran a hand over her belly.

"She's due in a month and she'll never get to meet him. How can that be so? I need to know how."

Sara inhaled a breath and reached for the woman's hand. "I'm so sorry, but José was attacked by two assailants not long after he left the gym. He didn't stand a chance. His injuries were fatal."

Sonia snatched her hand away and covered her face as the tears flowed freely. Soon she rocked back and forth, making a hissing sound. Her breathing had changed now, and Sara was concerned about the baby. *What if she goes into labour because of the shock?*

"Are you all right, Sonia?"

"No. Yes. No, I don't think I'll ever be okay again."

"Do you need medical help? Is it the baby?"

"I don't know. I have pains in my tummy, worse than I've ever experienced before."

Sara fished her mobile out of her pocket and rang nine-nine-nine. "Hello, I need an ambulance. I'm DI Sara Ramsey. I have an eight-month-pregnant woman with me, I think she's gone into labour. Please hurry." Sara gave the operator the woman's name and address.

"Okay, Inspector. An ambulance has been dispatched. I need you to stay on the line with me until they get there. Is Sonia in any danger?"

"Not imminent, no. I'm out of my depth here. I've never had children so I don't know what to do or what to expect."

"It's okay. That's what I'm here for. Just stay with Sonia and comfort her."

"How long is the ambulance likely to be?" Sara asked, anxiety clawing at her stomach.

"Another fifteen minutes or so. Not too long now. You're doing exceptionally well. Does Sonia have a member of her family close by?"

"She wants to know if you have family living near here."

"No. They're on the other side of Hereford, out towards Malvern. At least thirty minutes away."

She relayed the reply to the operator.

"Don't worry. We can contact them later." The operator kept

checking how Sonia was off and on and finally announced, "The ambulance is two minutes away now."

Sara strained her ears for any sign of the siren. "Should I go to the door to meet them? What about leaving Sonia on her own?"

"Can you hear them coming?"

"No, I can't. Not yet... no, wait. I think I can now." Sara left the sofa and raced to the window. She peered to the right first, nothing, and then to the left. There, in the distance, the night sky was lit up by flashing blue lights and the siren was getting louder by the second.

Sonia moaned.

Sara shot back to the sofa and bent down. "They're here now. Stay calm, everything is going to be okay, Sonia."

"Are they there?" the operator asked.

Sara rushed out into the hallway. "Yes, I'm just opening the front door for them, presuming the ambulance is for us and not a neighbour."

"You can safely assume that to be the case. As soon as they arrive, hang up and I'll leave you to deal with the paramedics."

"Thanks for all your help. They've drawn up outside."

"Okay. We can end the call now. Good luck, and thank you for being there with her."

"It's all part of the job," Sara lowered her voice and added, "I had to tell her that her husband had lost his life tonight. The shock sent her into labour."

"Oh my, I'm not surprised. It's a difficult phase in her pregnancy."

"I hope the baby survives."

"It should do. You acted quickly. You should be proud of yourself, especially if you're inexperienced at this lark."

"Thanks. It's my duty, I suppose."

"Something to put on your CV anyway."

Two male paramedics tore out of the vehicle. One carried a large medical bag.

"Is she okay?" the first paramedic asked.

"I think she's gone into labour. I had to share bad news with her, and this was her reaction."

Both men stopped. "What news, can you tell us?"

"Hurry, we don't have time for this," Sara insisted.

Both men rose to the challenge and rushed past Sara and into the house.

"First room you come to," she called from behind. By this stage, her adrenaline was pumping furiously through her veins. She followed the two men into the lounge.

Sonia cried out with relief when she saw them and explained that she thought her waters had broken. "I want my husband," she cried out.

The first paramedic glanced at Sara as if to ask where he was, and she shook her head. He rolled his eyes and took over, talking to the woman, bombarding her with instructions, to get her mind off the terrible fact that her husband wasn't able to be there at what should have been one of the greatest pleasures in her life.

The other paramedic whizzed past Sara again to retrieve the stretcher. Sonia was placed on it and wheeled out to the ambulance.

"Please, please, you have to ring my mother. Tell her I'm on the way to hospital."

Sara called after Sonia, "Where do I find her number?"

"In my bag. It's in the kitchen. Please bring it to me."

On the hunt for the elusive handbag, Sara bolted through the house and found it sitting on the worktop in the kitchen. She grabbed it and ran out to the ambulance.

Sonia took it and plunged a hand inside to retrieve her mobile just as a strong contraction hit her. Sonia dropped her bag, spilling the contents.

Sara found the phone and handed it to Sonia. "Open it and I'll search for your mother's number."

Sonia struggled as she clearly fought the urge to throw the phone at Sara. She handed it back and said, "Just press one, that's Mum's designated number."

"Okay, leave it with me."

Sara leapt out of the ambulance, and the paramedics proceeded to strap Sonia in, ready for the journey. "Sorry, what's your mother's name?" she asked, her mind still in a confused whirl.

"Eileen Fisher."

Sara jabbed the number one and waited for the call to be answered.

"Hello, love. It's late for you to be calling."

"Hello, Mrs Fisher. This is DI Sara Ramsey. I'm with your daughter right now, actually, she's on her way to Hereford Hospital. We believe she's gone into labour," Sara babbled, not allowing the woman to interject.

"Oh my. But she's early. Fred, get your shoes on. Sonia has gone into labour. Is she okay?"

"At the moment, yes. There's something else I need to make you aware of."

Mrs Fisher gasped. "What's that?"

Sara turned her back on Sonia and whispered, "José died this evening."

Mrs Fisher screamed. "No. That can't be right. How? Oh my God!"

"What the hell is wrong with you now?" a man's voice bellowed.

"José is dead. That's probably why she's gone into labour."

"Shit!" the man shouted in response.

"I'm going to have to go now. Shall I tell Sonia you're on your way?"

"Yes. We'll be leaving as soon as we get our coats and shoes on. Thank you for ringing us."

"You're welcome. Please, drive carefully."

"We will."

Sara placed the phone back in Sonia's bag. "They'll meet you there."

"Thank you," Sonia said through her tears. "Were they okay?"

"Yes, they're concerned about you. I told them about José, I hope I did the right thing?"

"You did."

"Right, we're ready for the off, Inspector," one of the paramedics said.

"Okay. I'll follow you there." She turned away and cringed. *Why the heck did I say that? It's almost ten, she's in safe hands, there's nothing I can do for her now. I should have said, 'I'll see you in the morning'. Me and my big mouth.*

"Please, there's no need for you to come. You look tired. I'm sure I'll be okay. Go home," Sonia asserted.

Sara smiled. "Are you sure?"

"I am." Just then another contraction caused Sonia to double over.

"I'll drop by in the morning to see how you are. I hope everything goes well with the birth."

"Thank you. Please, the only way you can help me now is by finding my husband's killer."

"I promise you, we're going to do our very best. Just concentrate on bringing the little one into the world safely."

"Is that it?" the paramedic asked. He inched the door closed, eager to get on the road. His colleague had settled himself into the seat in the back, next to Sonia.

"My apologies for holding you up. I'm done here."

"You haven't." He slammed the door shut.

"Take care of her," Sara shouted.

"We will. Good luck with your investigation."

Sara smiled and went back to the house to secure the door. Then she sat in her car and took a few breaths for a while. The time was now ten-fifteen, and she was dead on her feet. She pushed herself and called Lorraine's number.

"Hello."

"It's Sara. Where are you?"

"I've just got on the road with a couple of members of my team. We're on our way to the second crime scene. Are you still there?"

"No. I left to inform the next of kin."

"Oh heck, I take it that didn't go as planned, judging by your tone."

"No, the wife is heavily pregnant and went into labour. I had to call an ambulance. They've just left."

"Damn. It must have been the shock. Hang on, I'm being slow on the uptake here... So that means you must have identified the victim. How?"

"The manager of the gym, not far from where he was murdered, he found him. I had a chat with him. José Hickman was a member there."

"Ah, that makes sense. Did he have a bust-up with one of the punters at the gym and get jumped outside or something?"

"Good guess, but no. The manager caught the attack on CCTV footage. I've got a copy of it. There were two assailants. The attack was brutal, so be warned. The victim is now blessed with an extra smile."

"Shit! Poor bloke. That's great that you've got the assailants on camera. Could you make them out?"

"Nope, there's a dodgy streetlight, you'll see for yourself soon enough. I've got the uniformed coppers carrying out the necessary door-to-door enquiries in the vicinity."

"Good thinking. Catch people while it's still fresh in their minds."

"That was my thinking, too. Hey, I'd love to come back to the crime scene to hold your hand, but the truth is, I'm knackered. Will you forgive me if I call it a day?"

"Sara, you don't answer to me. You've gone above and beyond tonight as it is. Go home, get some rest, and we'll catch up tomorrow."

"See, I feel guilty doing that, knowing that you'll still be plodding on while I'm tucked up in bed."

"You missed out that you'll be spooning in bed with that hunk of a husband of yours."

Sara laughed. She hadn't done much of that during the day. "If you say so. I'll send him your best regards."

"Yeah, okay. Also tell him if he's ever at a loose end in the evening, you know, if you're out pounding the streets anytime, to give me a call."

"You cheeky bitch. Hey, you're forgetting that if I'm out on the street it's usually because you've called me to attend a crime scene."

"Ah, I knew you'd pick up the flaw in my statement, eventually."

"I guess I must be more tired than I thought. I'm going now. I'll speak to you in the morning, Lorraine. Don't work too hard."

"I'll work as hard as necessary, it's not as if I'm fortunate enough to have someone at home awaiting my arrival, is it?"

"See, you've done it again. Made me feel guilty for the second time this evening."

"Stop talking shit and go. That's an order."

"Yes, ma'am. Take care."

"Drive safely."

Sara jabbed the End Call button and threw her mobile on the seat beside her. She took a few seconds' time out to rest her head against the steering wheel to gather the strength to drive home. Then she started the car and began her journey. She rang Mark on the way, hoping that he wouldn't be tucked up in bed.

He sounded pleased to hear from her, which was a bonus she hadn't been expecting. She used the siren to get home quicker when the traffic hit a bad patch on the edge of the town.

Ten minutes later, she walked into Mark's arms at her front door. Her emotions overwhelmed her. She hugged him tightly and sobbed.

"Hey, what's all this?" Mark shuffled them inside and closed the door.

"I'm shattered. However, the thought of us falling out has had a devastating effect on me all evening."

"Did we? Fall out? I'm aware of me unnecessarily giving you a hard time, but I certainly didn't intend for you to think we'd fallen out. I regret bitching about your job. You should have ignored me."

She sniffled and looked up at him. "How could I ignore you? If you have doubts about my career affecting our relationship then we should sit down and discuss it properly."

"Now you're talking nonsense. It was an off-the-cuff whine, nothing serious. I've been sitting here stewing over it while you've been out."

She kissed him, long and hard. "I'm so glad we can discuss our differences and sort things out."

"I'll work on my side a bit better. I've hated myself all evening. Misty sensed something was wrong as well, her cuddles have been non-existent since you left. She went up to bed about an hour ago. I think she's sulking."

Sara chuckled. "She's adorable and so are you. I need a drink to unwind, it's been a hell of a night."

"I'll get you one. Do you want to take it up to bed?"

"You read my mind."

"Go on up, I'll fix the drinks and join you."

"I'm going to have a quick shower first. Get the smell of death off me."

Mark wrinkled his nose and kissed her on the cheek. "I couldn't do your job, not in a million years."

"Yeah, tonight's cases were exceptionally brutal."

He stepped out of the hug and walked into the kitchen. "Go, I'll bring them up in a second."

Sara clung on to the banister and hauled herself up the stairs. She glanced up and saw Misty standing at the top, rubbing herself against the newel post. "Hello, you." She picked up her cat and snuggled into her fur. "I've missed you this evening."

Misty rubbed her head against Sara's and then struggled to get out of her arms and flew down the stairs. "Misty is on her way down. Can you let her out, please, Mark?"

"Leave her to me."

She continued into the bedroom and stripped off. Once in the shower, she turned up the temperature and lifted her face to the spray, allowing it to ease the strain and stresses that had blighted her throughout the day.

Mark was waiting in bed when she emerged a little while later. Misty had forgiven him and was now snuggled up for a cute cuddle. She slipped into bed beside them both.

"I forgot to ask, did you ring the hospital for me to find out how Mum was?"

"I did. They said she was resting well. Your father hasn't left her side all day, though, the nurse was a little concerned about his welfare. I told her we'd sort out some kind of rota between us, make sure he gets a break."

Sara shook her head. "I'm warning you now, he won't listen. He's a stubborn old fox. He'll see it as his duty to be beside her during her stay in hospital."

"Then it's up to us to try and persuade him otherwise, isn't it?"

"We can try. I'll give Lesley a call in the morning. See what we can organise."

As soon as her head sank into the pillow, her eyelids became heavy and impossible to keep open. She took a sip from her drink and then drifted off to sleep, ignoring the rest of it.

7

The next day Sara ached all over, feeling a darn sight older than her thirty-five years. She came downstairs to find Mark busy in the kitchen, fixing her breakfast. Her stomach rumbled with the aroma of fried bacon and sausages. "Are you spoiling me again?"

"You're worth spoiling. You can't go to work on an empty stomach. Sit down, I'm about to dish up."

Sara glided across the kitchen and pecked him on the cheek. "I'll be forever grateful for the day you walked into my life. Not just because you cook the best breakfast this side of the Malvern Hills, but because you're the most selfless person I know."

"Get out of here. All I'm doing is watching out for the amazing woman who agreed to marry me."

He leaned in to kiss her, and then he shooed her away. "Go and sit yourself down."

Sara didn't speak again until she pushed her empty plate away. Washing her fry-up down with a cup of coffee had truly set her up for the day. "That was delicious. I hope I stay awake long enough to hold the morning meeting when I get there."

"You'll be fine, you're always the consummate professional where work is concerned."

"Have you got much on today?"

"A few castrations and a broken leg to mend, that should see me through to lunchtime. Talking of which, I should get out of here. Not nagging you, just a friendly reminder that you said you'd call Lesley this morning to sort out some kind of rota with her."

"Thanks. I hadn't forgotten. I thought I'd do it on the way into work, probably while I'm stuck in the rush hour traffic. I just hope she's up. She can be such a grouch if I wake her up too early. I'll do the dishes and then get on the road."

"No, you won't, leave it to me. I'll quickly see to them before I shoot off."

"You're an absolute gem. No idea what I ever did to deserve you being part of my life."

They shared a greasy kiss. Sara had a quick cuddle with Misty and then flew out of the house, not knowing when she'd see the inside of it again, if yesterday's shenanigans were anything to go by.

Mark waved her off. She pulled onto the main road in Hereford and prepared herself for the anticipated telling off she was about to receive for calling her sister before nine o'clock.

"Hi, Lesley, it's me."

"I can see that. What do you want at this ungodly hour... oh no, it's not Mum, is it?"

"No, she's fine, as far as I know. That's my next call. Sorry to wake you. Mark and I were discussing what to do about Mum last night, and he came up with the idea of going to see her on some kind of rota. That way we give Dad a break from sitting there all day and all night."

"It would be pointless. Dad wants to be with her. You're not going to get him to leave her bedside, I'm telling you that now."

"I know it's going to be difficult, but it's up to us to force him to take better care of himself. He'll be no good to Mum if he gets ill, will he?"

"I'm fully aware of that. I'm telling you, he won't listen. I doubt it. We're not going to be able to prise him away from her bedside. So there's little point in us trying."

Sara blew out a frustrated breath. Deep down, she knew her sister was right, but there was a determination roaring inside her to do the right thing by her father. "Can we at least try? He might surprise us all and give in, if we all peck at him enough."

"There again, it's possible he might blow his top and stop us from visiting Mum, full stop."

"Shit. There is that. This is so difficult, we both know how stubborn he is. When we were there yesterday, he seemed as frail as Mum at one stage."

"I noticed that as well. Leave it with me. I'm off work for the next couple of days, I'm sure you've got enough on your plate as it is."

"Thanks, sis. Four deaths this week alone. However, you only have to say the word and I'll drop everything and come running, you hear me?"

"I know you will. I'll give you a call if Mum's condition deteriorates, I promise. Now let me get back to sleep for half an hour or so."

"You and your bed, you're not often parted from it, are you?" Sara laughed.

"Not if I can help it. Are you going to ring the hospital?"

"Yep, about to do it now. I'll speak to you later. Thanks for always being there for me, Lesley."

"Ditto. Try to have a stress-free day."

"Ha, some hope of that happening." She ended the call and then immediately dialled the hospital. One of the nurses told her that her mother was asleep after having a restless night. They had upped her pain medication at around three, allowing her to sleep. "How's my father?"

"He's tired, he's barely slept all night, worried about your mother. He dropped off at around six this morning and had about two hours' sleep. We've tried to persuade him to go to the canteen, but he's having none of it."

"I've just called my sister, she's going to pop in soon to give him a break. It might be better coming from a member of staff, though. I don't think he's likely to listen to us."

"I'll have a word with the ward sister, see if she can have a discussion with him about watching his own health doesn't deteriorate."

"That would be wonderful. Unfortunately, I'm at work all day, however, if Mum should get any worse, will someone ring me?"

"Are you the police officer?"

"That's right."

"We've got your phone number. I'll make sure someone contacts you straight away. She's in safe hands. Try not to cause yourself any unnecessary stress, you have an important job to carry out."

"Thanks for understanding. I'd better go now."

"Take care."

After ending the call, she contemplated what life was possibly going to be like without her mother around. The truth was, she couldn't. Tears blurred her vision the rest of the way into the city centre. She pulled into the station car park, wiped her nose and eyes with a tissue and then ventured inside.

Carla caught her up on the stairs. "Hey, didn't you hear me shouting your name?"

"Sorry, I was in a world of my own. How are you?"

"I'm fine. Crikey, you look like death warmed up. Not bad news about your mum, I hope."

"No, she's plodding on. A bit of a rough night, but the nurses upped her medication."

"I'm so sorry, Sara. Did you have trouble sleeping yourself last night?"

"No, I slept like a log. Let's just say I had an eventful evening. I'll tell you all about it during the morning meeting."

"Sounds ominous. You're not going to tell us you're jacking it in, are you?"

Sara stopped halfway up the stairs. "What gives you that idea?"

"You seem hacked off."

"A lot you know. I'm tired, that's all. Two days running I've pulled a fourteen- to fifteen-hour shift."

"What are you talking about?"

They continued the climb to the top. Sara pushed open the door to the incident room and headed towards the whiteboard. She picked up the marker pen and scribbled the two names of the latest victims on the board. Carla took the hint and put her hand in her pocket to buy the first coffees of the day.

Her partner placed the cup on the desk beside Sara. "You should have rung me."

"Why? There was nothing you could have done."

Over the next five minutes or so, the rest of the team filtered in. Sara left the incident room, hung her coat up in the office, glanced sideways at the paperwork littering her desk and walked out again. *Sod that for a lark, the mindless paperwork can wait.*

"All right, now we're all here, I want to give you the lowdown on what happened last night. Then we'll assess where both ongoing cases are and work out what we do to divide the workload up going forward."

"You mean you're expecting us to spread ourselves even more, to cope with these two new cases?" Carla asked, disbelief etched into her expression.

"Hear me out, Carla. I know it's going to put us under immense pressure, but all four victims deserve justice in my opinion."

"Whoa, I'm not disagreeing with you, but four separate bloody cases at once? There's no way any team could cope with that, boss. Not in a million years."

"We've done it before, and I have every faith in you guys."

"Can I just remind you about what you told me on the way in? That you've put in two fifteen-hour days on the trot?"

"You don't need to remind me, my body is aware of the punishment I've dished out lately. We can do this."

"Can we? Is the Super going to grant us overtime? Gone are the days I give the force a couple of free hours' work a day, especially when it's not appreciated by HQ."

Sara shuffled her feet. "I hear what you're saying. That's why we need to split up and work methodically."

Carla raised an eyebrow and shook her head. "The way we work every day of the week we show up here, you mean?"

"Yes. Come on, Carla, don't put a negative spin on this before I've even divulged what I was faced with last night."

"Believe me, I'm trying not to, but it isn't easy, knowing the pressure we're under already."

"Just hear me out." Sara ploughed on. "Right, the first case is that of a victim found in a burned-out car. Lorraine believes the victim's hands were tied to the steering wheel and some form of accelerant was used to finish him off, probably petrol."

"Wouldn't the flames get rid of any likely evidence?" Craig asked.

"Yes. Luckily, Lorraine found a snippet of a plastic tie in the footwell beneath the steering wheel, hence her conclusion that the man was tied up before he perished."

Sara circled the victim's name. "Does anybody recognise this name?"

Carla frowned and inclined her head. "Kind of. Should we? Is he a prominent figure?"

"None other than one of the top prosecuting solicitors in the area."

Craig and Barry both let out a long, low whistle.

Sara nodded. "Exactly. Anyway, putting that to one side for a moment or two, I was attending the crime scene when I received another call from the control room, regarding a second victim." She circled José Hickman's name. "He was found in a dimly lit alley by the manager of the gym he had gone to last night. Here's the thing, the manager caught the attack on camera." She waved the disc she had taken out of her handbag. "Two attackers. I've watched it. I cringed all the way through it. They swooped, did the deed and left him lying there with his throat cut wide open."

"Do you want me to run the disc, boss?" Craig asked, ever the eager team member.

"Why not? You can see for yourselves what we're up against with this one."

Craig pounced on the disc and worked his magic with the equipment. Within a few seconds, they were all watching the murder play out on the huge TV screen. Even though Sara was aware of what was about to happen, and when, she still winced, she couldn't help it. The attack was brutal and vicious. Sara glanced around the team.

"Two assailants, doesn't that ring a bell?" Craig asked.

It wasn't until Craig mentioned it that Sara twigged what he was getting at. She clicked her thumb and middle finger together. "You're right." She turned back to the whiteboard and circled the second victim. "The two on the bike. Although, it could be a coincidence."

Craig shrugged. "Maybe."

She nodded. "Worth the shout, though, Craig. We'll bear it in mind. It might make sense to lump the two cases together to investigate. What do you say, Christine and Marissa?"

The two women looked at each other and nodded. "Sounds good to us, boss," Christine replied. "Should we chase up forensics, see if they found anything on the bike?"

"Good idea. I doubt it, after it being dumped in the river. Okay, that means the rest of us can focus on the Pittman and the Chaddock cases. Or would you ladies rather have someone else on your team?" she asked Christine and Marissa, aware that there were four of them on the first and third cases.

"Shall we leave things as they are for now, boss?" Marissa said. "We can always give you a shout if we get overwhelmed."

"Okay, make sure you do. I think the Miles Chaddock case is going to be a pain in the backside. Carla and I will be paying his workplace a visit right after this meeting. Going back to last night's events. I've already made Miles Chaddock's wife aware of his death. When I interviewed her, she couldn't tell me anything, unfortunately. Hence our trip to the office this morning. As far as José is concerned, when I dropped by his house to notify his wife, the woman was heavily pregnant and went into labour. That reminds me, I need to chase up her welfare this morning before we set off. Again, I tried to interview her but it didn't go well. From what I could gather, she struggled to come up with any idea why someone should want to kill her husband. I only got so far with the interview before the baby began to announce its entrance into the world. Is everyone clear on their tasks for the day? With regard to the first two cases, we need to keep up our pace with those at the same time."

When no one else raised any viable points, Sara drew the meeting to a close and went into her office. She peered out at the dull skies overshadowing the city and switched on the light. "It kind of reflects my mood today," she muttered on the way to her desk.

"Are you talking to yourself again?" Carla said from the doorway.

"Sorry, I didn't realise you were spying on me."

"Ouch! That was below the belt, even for you. What do you want me to do?"

"Nothing at the moment. Just be ready to go once I've checked in at the hospital about Sonia. It might warrant a trip to see her later on this afternoon."

"Oh great. We seem to spend all our time there lately." Carla cringed and bit down on her lip. "Me and my big mouth, sorry."

"It's fine. I didn't think anything of it. Actually, either Christine or Marissa can go."

"Dare I ask the inevitable question? How's your mum really doing, you were a tad evasive on the way in?"

"She had a rough night. They had to tinker with her pain meds, but she fell asleep after that. It's Dad who I'm more concerned about. He hasn't left her side."

"That's not good. Are the hospital feeding him?"

"I doubt it. Lesley is going over there this morning, she'll force him to eat something, knowing her, but I can't see him going home to get changed anytime soon."

"What a terrible situation. I can understand him not wanting to leave your mother, they're soulmates, aren't they?"

"Yeah. I dread to think what's going to happen to him once she passes away." Tears threatened, and she waved her hand. "Don't start me off, I'm trying to keep my mind occupied so I don't think about it."

"I think I'd be the same. I'm always here if you need to vent or want a shoulder to cry on. Lord knows the boot has been on the other foot enough times in the last year or so."

"Thank God all that's in the past and you have a caring fella in your life now."

"This is probably a bad time…"

Sara cocked her head, concerned. "Go on."

"Des and I were chatting last night and, before you say it, we're aware how loved-up we are, anyway, I digress. Lorraine's name cropped up. Or rather her dating dilemma."

Sara blew out a breath. "Why am I sensing that I'm not going to like this?"

"Wait, it's good, I promise you."

"All right, I'm listening. Go on."

"We think we've got the ideal solution to her problem."

"Surprise me. What have you come up with?"

"Des's good friend, Paul, he's recently been through a dreadful divorce. He's looking to get back into the dating scene."

Sara's mouth twisted. "Have you vetted him? I don't mean that nastily, but Des's idea of a perfect match might not be ours."

"Cynic. I'll be meeting him properly at the weekend. Des has asked him over for dinner on Saturday."

"Where does he live?"

"In Worcester, but I think he's keen on a move to Hereford. He and Des are best friends and tend to be tied at the hip."

"Ugh... sounds like a warning bell should be ringing in respect to your relationship, hon."

"He's fine from what I can gather."

"How many times have you met him?"

Carla smiled. "Twice. Only fleetingly, but he was the perfect gent on both occasions."

"Glad to hear it. Cheeky request, have you got a photo of him?"

Carla dipped out of the office and returned scrolling through her phone. "Let's see. Ah yes, here it is."

Sara studied the man's features. He had slightly thinning hair and a kind face. "He seems okay. Is he a copper?"

"Yes, how could you tell?"

"There's just something about him. My advice would be to get to know him a little better at the weekend and then decide if you think we should pursue introducing him to Lorraine."

"Good idea. Okay, I know how busy you are, I'll leave you to it."

"While I'm on the phone to the hospital, see what you can find out about Miles Chaddock for me."

"I'll do my best."

Sara rang the number for the hospital and asked to be put through to the Maternity Unit. "Hi, I'm DI Ramsey. I'm calling to enquire how Sonia Hickman is."

"Oh, yes. She's doing really well. Is this a personal call?"

"Not really. You're aware of what happened to her husband, I take it?"

"I am. An absolute tragedy for the poor woman."

"Can I ask how she seems to be coping with the news?"

"She has her moments. I think having her cherished baby to consider now has probably been a blessing in disguise."

"Would it be an imposition for me to come and have a chat with her?"

"About the crime?"

"Yes. Or do you think I should leave it a few days?"

"My expert opinion would be to leave her alone for a while, but I'm sure she would want to speak to you and help with your investigation."

"It's a tough call to make, isn't it? Would you mind asking her if she wants to see me now?"

"I'll be right back, hold the line."

Sara fed a pen through her fingers while she waited. It wasn't long before the nurse returned and told her, "Hi, yes, Sonia said to come in when you want. She's eager to have a chat with you."

"That's great. I have an important visit to make first. I'll drop in later, if that's all right? Any times I should avoid coming?"

"No, not at all. Come when you want."

"Thanks for your help." Sara hung up and left the office.

Carla was working on her computer. She hit one of the keys enthusiastically, and the printer churned into life, spewing out several sheets of paper.

Sara stopped by the machine and picked up one of the sheets and read it. "Wow, are these all the cases he's prosecuted?"

"Yes, I went back five years, is that enough?"

"It'll do for now. Let's take them with us, you can read some out to me while I drive."

"Or I could drive and you could spend the time reading through the notes."

"Smart alec. You've got a deal. We'll take my car."

"If we have to," Carla complained good-naturedly. She unhooked her jacket from the back of the chair, and they left the incident room.

*T*en minutes later, they drew up outside Bartholomew's Solicitors in the centre of the city.

"According to the number of cases he's had this year alone, he was an exceptionally busy man," Sara said.

"It's a shame he's now dead. We need more prosecutors of his calibre."

"Ain't that the truth?" Sara clawed at the handle to open the door, but her mobile rang, preventing her from exiting the car. She glanced at the caller ID, and Lorraine's name filled the tiny screen. "Hey, you. What time did you crawl into bed last night?"

"This morning, you mean. Around two-fifteen, I think it was."

"Oh, bugger. Deal a girl a guilty blow, why don't you?"

"Nonsense. We all have our crosses to bear. Just do me one thing."

"Name it."

"Catch the bastard killing these people."

Sara's brow furrowed. "You say that as though you know who is behind all these murders. Do you?"

"Nope, I haven't got the foggiest. I do have a snippet of information that I think will help, though."

"What's that?"

"While searching through the victims' personal items, all four of them had something in common. Sorry, correction, three of them... no, as you were, it is all four of them."

"What? Are you winding me up? And what's that?"

"Each of them had a business card for Bartholomew's Solicitors."

Sara gasped. "We're on our way there now. That's where Miles Chaddock worked."

"That's why I dithered about saying it was all four victims with the cards. It goes without saying that he would carry one in his own wallet."

"Bloody hell. So all the cases are linked? We needn't split them up? In other words, you're telling me we should be treating this as a serial killer case."

"Yep, I suppose that's what it amounts to. Don't you agree?"

"Okay. I suppose during the morning meeting we were halfway there with that conclusion after we figured out that two of the victims were killed by two killers."

"That thought crossed my mind as soon as the business cards came to light."

Something in the back of Sara's mind was bugging her. She switched off from the conversation for a moment to try and make sense of things. *There's something there, but what?*

"Sara, are you still with me?" Lorraine asked impatiently.

"Sorry. Yes, I'm here. You know when you've heard a snippet of information and discounted it at the time, only for it to bug you a little while later? Well, that's what I'm trying to make sense of right now... oh shit, I've got it." She groaned, and her heart thumped against her ribs. "It was last night, something the gym manager told me. I dismissed it at the time, but now... now it's all making perfect sense to me, sort of."

"You're waffling. What are you trying to say, Sara?" Lorraine pressed.

Sara faced Carla and punched her forehead. "I'm so stupid at times."

Carla shook her head. "You're not. Maybe you've been off your game since you heard the news about your mum, but that was to be expected."

"Am I no longer included in this conversation?" Lorraine demanded.

Sara exhaled a breath. "Sorry. Okay, here's what I have for you. It was last night, when I was interviewing the manager of the gym. He told me in passing that José Hickman had been on jury service recently."

"What the actual fuck!" Lorraine shouted. "You need to do some digging. See if all the other victims were on the same jury. If they were, then that's the missing part of the puzzle."

"Jesus, I hate to be the bearer of bad news, but apart from the solicitor, we have three other victims, that leaves another nine people left on that jury, if what you're thinking is right," Carla pointed out.

"She's got a point," Lorraine chipped in.

"Okay, I've got to go, Lorraine. I'll be in touch soon. Thanks for the information."

"My pleasure. Go get 'em, tiger." Lorraine ended the call.

"I need to let the team know before we go inside." Sara rang the station, and Christine answered. "Christine, I need you to listen very carefully. I've just come off the phone with the pathologist. She's informed me she believes all four victims are connected."

"Wowza, so we can combine resources again now, is that it?"

"Yes. There's more. Last night, the manager of the gym told me that José Hickman had recently been on jury duty. I need you to ring the families of the other victims, or as many as you can get hold of, and ask if the vics had also been on jury duty in the last few months."

"Blimey, that's way out there. We'll get to it right away, boss."

"Wait. I know this is going to involve a lot of work for you but I need you to then try and find out who the other members of that jury were. That should keep you busy until we get back. We'll do our best to try and source as much information as we can at this end."

"Leave it with me. We'll work our socks off as usual, don't worry."

"I know you will."

Sara pressed the End Call button and slipped her phone into her pocket. "Let's get this over with. I hope they don't dig their heels in and refuse to give us the information."

"There's every chance that's going to happen."

They left the vehicle and entered the solicitor's office. A brunette receptionist with crooked teeth greeted them.

Sara and Carla flashed their IDs. "DI Ramsey and DS Jameson. We'd like to speak to the person in charge on an urgent police matter, please."

"Oh, okay. Let me see if Miss Watson is available to see you." She left her desk and trotted up the hallway. She returned a few moments later with a slim redhead in tow.

"You wanted to see me?"

Sara introduced herself and Carla again. "We're here to discuss a colleague of yours, if you have a spare moment."

"Sounds intriguing. Why don't you come into my office?"

"Thanks, we'd appreciate that."

They followed Miss Watson back up the hallway and into a large plush office. Bookcases lined the far wall, and on the opposite wall was a set of French doors that led out to a pretty courtyard area.

"Please, don't be shy, take a seat. You alluded to this meeting being about a colleague of mine. Would you be talking about Miles Chaddock?"

"That's right. I take it his wife has been in touch this morning."

"Yes, to say I was shocked by the revelation would be a gross understatement. Are you the officer leading the investigation?"

"That's right. This week we've been called out to four murder scenes. It's just come to light that we believe all four victims were loosely connected."

"My goodness. May I ask in what way?"

"A throwaway comment at one of the scenes yesterday has led me to believe that possibly three of the victims might have been on jury duty together and possibly that Miles Chaddock was the prosecuting solicitor."

Miss Watson's mouth dropped open, and she sprang forward in her seat. Recovering from the disclosure, she asked, "What? Are you sure?"

"Not one hundred percent, no. But my team are delving into the probability as we speak. Three of the victims had one of your firm's business cards in their possession at the time of their death. Is it normal for you to dish out cards to jurors?"

Her brow wrinkled. "Our solicitors are asked to do so, but only at the very end of a trial, never during or before."

"That answers that query then. I presume for you to obtain any future business, correct?"

"Yes. We saw one of our competitors doing the very same last year and felt there was nothing wrong in it, so jumped in feet first."

"That makes perfect sense to me. What I need to know is if you'd be prepared to speak openly with us regarding Miles Chaddock's recent cases. We did a quick search on the internet and printed out a list; what we need to know is whether the list is up to date."

"Of course. I'll be open and truthful with you if there's a chance it will lead to a conviction. I'll need to call on my assistant to help me obtain the information you're seeking, would that be okay?"

"Of course. Do what you need to do. Also, maybe we should actually start by asking if Miles ever complained that he had been threatened by someone he was prosecuting?"

She glanced at the wall behind Sara and contemplated her answer for a moment or two. "The reason for me pausing is that we all receive threats in one way or another. You only have to look at all our associates' inboxes to see what kind of pressure we're put under in that respect, on a daily basis. Most of the time we choose to ignore them, but there are instances when we feel the need to inform the police."

"Quite right, too. And are these emails taken seriously by my colleagues?"

"Yes, most of the time. Usually, an official warning is enough to ward off any future harassment."

"That's reassuring to know. Tell me, do you keep a note of the jurors who sit on each case that passes through these offices?"

"Yes, all the time. Any idea which case we could be talking about?"

"No, not at the moment. All we can give you are the names of the other victims we're dealing with, if that will help?"

"Let me get my assistant, she's our resident computer geek—sorry, I should say, expert." She flew out of her chair and exited the room.

"I'm excited about this," Carla leaned in and whispered.

"Me, too. Glad something is finally going our way."

"She doesn't seem that upset about Miles' death, does she?"

"I think we should give her a break. In my opinion, she seems eager to help us solve the cases. Maybe it'll hit her later, when she's at home. She also seems to be a consummate professional."

"Possibly. I'll give her the benefit of the doubt for now." Carla grinned.

Sara shook her head. "You're nuts."

"What happens when we get the information? Where do we go from there?"

"We're going to need to formulate a plan. We might need to call on extra resources to protect the rest of the jurors while we try to track down the killers."

"Easy, eh?"

"Hardly, however, it's got to be done."

Miss Watson came back into the room with a young blonde lady. "This is Ellie. If you tell her what you need, I'm sure she'll be able to accommodate you."

"Hi, Ellie. You're aware of the situation, I take it?"

Ellie nodded and smiled weakly. "Yes, poor Mr Chaddock."

"It's very sad. We have three other victims connected to his case. We're going to do our best to find the culprits and prevent any more lives being taken."

"Let's ensure that happens. Where do we start, Ellie?" Miss Watson said.

"If you give me the names of the three victims, I can input those into the system and see what comes up."

Sara took her notebook from her pocket and scribbled down the names then tore the sheet off and handed it to Ellie.

"Thanks, I'll do it in my office. Hopefully I should have some news for you soon."

8

$\mathcal{D}$es needed to visit the gents' loo before he hit the road. Feeling the urge to use the cubicle rather than the urinal, he closed the door behind him.

The main door squeaked open. He hated using the cubicles when someone else was around because of the implications. Everyone knew you only used the proper loo when you wanted a dump.

"I've told you to fucking stop panicking. No, Miles didn't deserve what became of him, but then neither did the others." The man sounded irate. He was trying hard to keep his voice down, but Des had excellent hearing.

His interest piqued when he heard the name Miles. *Where have I heard the name before?*

"Get a bloody grip, we've got others to deal with yet. You going off on one every five minutes isn't sodding helping. Mona, will you bloody listen to yourself…? No, I will not stop having a dig at you. We're in this… yes, up to our necks."

The outer door closed. Des wondered what the hell he'd just been privy to. He finished his ablutions and flushed the loo. He was desperate to get out there and see whose conversation he'd been listening to.

But first he needed to wash his hands. At the sink, he quickly ran through the 'Happy Birthday' song and dried his hands on his trousers. Peering out into the hallway, he saw it was clear. He slammed a fist against his leg and headed for the main entrance.

As he turned the corner, he found Detective Warren Finch blocking his path. "Where do you think you're going?"

"What's it to you, Finch?"

Finch's hand latched on to his throat. He dragged Des into the nearest available room and switched on the light. "You and I are going to have a little chat."

"About what?" Des was glad he'd just got off the loo, otherwise he sensed his trousers might have been full by now after recognising Finch's voice as the one on the phone in the toilet.

"Don't give me that bullshit. It was you in the toilet just a minute ago, wasn't it?"

"Yeah, I just had a shit, what about it?"

"You overheard my conversation, didn't you?"

"What conversation? You know what it's like, man, when you're having a dump, there's only one thing on your mind."

Finch's brow creased heavily. "You fucking pulling my dick, arsehole?"

"Not in the slightest. What's going on?"

Finch removed his hand from Des's throat and took a step back. "If I find out you've used any of that information against me... let's just say I know where you live."

"Meaning what? Bearing in mind I didn't hear anything and I don't have a clue what you're on about, man."

Finch wagged his finger. "Don't try and fuck with me. You're new here, aren't you?"

Des shrugged. "Yep, just trying to fit in the best way I can, and minding my own business is part of the process. You might not be aware of this, but I'm slightly deaf in one ear. I didn't hear a thing I shouldn't have heard."

Finch brushed himself down and glared at him. "One slip-up, and I'll nail your sorry arse to the cathedral wall, got it?"

"Yep, I hear you loud and clear... well, on this side anyway. It's a fucking nuisance having a dodgy ear. No idea how I passed the medical back in the day." He laughed and moved away from the wall.

Finch was on him in a flash and pinned him up against it again. "Don't go treating me like an idiot."

"Wouldn't dream of it, mate. I'm on a call-out, my partner is going to wonder where I am if I don't leave the building in the next five minutes."

Finch's gaze burrowed into his. Des resisted the urge to swallow down the acidic liquid burning his throat.

"You can go with this warning, mate. I'll be keeping a close eye on you in the future."

Des shrugged. "Whatever. I've done nothing wrong. Like I said, I'm just trying to fit in around here. Sorry if you think I've stepped on your toes."

Warren glowered at him and then pushed him in the back. "Get out of my sight, moron."

9

Sara and Carla returned to the station laden with paperwork to sift through that they knew would keep them busy for the rest of the day. A few hours in, and they had found the addresses of the rest of the jurors who had sat on a case in which notorious villain, Roger Barrett, had been convicted and sentenced to twenty years for numerous crimes, including murder, GBH, drug dealing and assaulting a police officer.

Carla searched the internet for the case, and they read through it together. "I roughly remember it. The hearing was held in a closed courtroom, apart from the jury in attendance."

Sara nodded. "It's coming back to me now. I recall something being circulated from HQ just before the trial, warning officers to be prepared for trouble. I believe he was ferried back and forth from the remand centre by armed police. The notion was that his men might attack and try to free him."

Carla sat back and placed her hands on her head. "That didn't come to fruition, so they thought they'd go around bumping off the jury instead, weeks after the trial had ended? Hard to bloody believe, isn't it?"

Sara shrugged. "It is. We need to trace the other gang members, put them under surveillance. They're obviously the ones behind the murders."

"One word: resources. We're snowed under as it is, what with these other high-profile cases taking place."

"I know. I didn't say it was going to be easy. I'll have a word with the chief, she needs to be aware of what we're up against. I'll be right back."

"Wait," Carla prevented her from leaving the office. "What do you want me to do in the meantime? I can't sit around, staring at this list and not doing anything."

"I know. My hands are tied until I run things past the chief. Bear with me for half an hour or so, things should be clearer by then, I hope."

Carla shrugged. "I just hate hanging around, especially when there are people out there in danger."

"Half an hour, tops. Be patient, partner."

Sara left the office and jogged along the corridor to DCI Price's office where the chief's efficient PA greeted her. "Sorry to be a pain in the rear, is there any chance I can see the chief urgently, Mary?"

"Take a seat. Let me see what I can do for you, Inspector Ramsey."

Instead of sitting, Sara paced the area until Mary came out of the office and nodded.

"Go right in. Can I get you a coffee?"

"Only if it's not putting you out."

Mary smiled. "It's not. I'll bring it in."

"You're amazing, I don't care what the chief says about you." Sara laughed and entered the office.

DCI Price set a file aside on her desk and sat upright. She gestured for Sara to take a seat. "Inspector, is something wrong?"

"I'd say plenty, boss." She gave the chief the lowdown on what they had so far on the four cases. The chief took the news in her stride at first, until Sara mentioned she needed extra resources to ensure the rest of the jury should be put under surveillance.

"You genuinely think this guy is running the show from prison?"

"One hundred percent. You know what these hard-nosed criminals are like. Maybe he got his goons to put pressure on the jury during the trial."

The chief thought over Sara's suggestion. "What, and then when it came to the crunch you think the jury backtracked, thinking they would be safe with the guy sitting behind bars?"

"Perhaps. I'm going to need to speak to one of them to see if anything like that went down. It seems feasible to me."

"Have you looked into what safe houses are available at this time?"

Sara sighed and shook her head. "I'm thinking there won't be any, not with the high-profile cases going on. We're stuck between a rock and a hard place, aren't we?"

"What do you suggest we do?"

"I was hoping you would give me some pointers, not the other way around."

"I'm sure if we put our heads together, we can come up with a possible solution soon."

Mary entered the room and handed them each a cup of coffee. The next five minutes were spent bouncing around different suggestions, only for all of them to be shot down in flames by the other.

"This is a tad out there, but we've dismissed every other viable option so far," Sara began.

The chief cocked an eyebrow. "I'm listening."

"What if we round up all the jurors and keep them safe in a large venue, manned by armed police?"

"Over the top, I agree. But then again, it's imperative that we keep these people safe. It's our duty, in fact. Like where?"

"I don't know, maybe a village hall, community centre, or even a church."

Carol sipped at her drink. "It could work. The logistics of such a scheme are going to be a nightmare to arrange. Saying that, if anyone is up to the job, then you're the person to do it."

Sara raised a finger. "Me and my expert team, you mean. My mind is still elsewhere, I can't see that changing anytime soon."

"Do you want me to draft in someone else from another area?"

"What? And let them take all the glory when we're the ones who have put in all the hard graft? Nope, I think Carla and I have it covered."

"Good. Is there anything you need me to do?"

Sara grinned. "You could run the idea past your contact at the Armed Response Unit, see what he makes of it. Maybe he'll know of a suitable location where we can hold them."

Nodding, Carol picked up her phone and dialled a number. "Leave it with me."

Sara smiled and left her seat, taking her cup of delicious coffee with her. "I couldn't leave this behind," she told Mary.

"Take a seat and finish it."

Although she was tempted, Sara knew it was imperative for her to get back to organise the logistical nightmare that lay ahead of them. "I'd better get back, Mary. Thank you for always brightening my day with a refreshing cuppa."

"You're more than welcome. Good luck, Inspector."

"Thanks, on this one, I think I'm going to need it."

On her way back to the incident room, Sara literally bumped into a distracted Des. "Hey, everything all right, Des?"

"Why? Shouldn't it be?" he snapped.

Sara inclined her head. "Something on your mind?"

He shook his head and mumbled something, then turned and walked away from her. The incident left Sara confused and with a surging dilemma. *Do I tell Carla or should I keep quiet about it? He seemed as if he had the weight of the world on his shoulders. I've not known him long but if I didn't know any better, I'd say he was under a huge amount of stress. Maybe he's not fitting in as well as he hoped. Strange, Carla hasn't mentioned that he's finding it difficult.*

She shrugged and continued on her journey. She decided to push her concerns about Des to the back of her mind, thinking she had enough shit to deal with at the moment. She entered the incident room, and a feeling of pride gushed through her. All members of her team had their heads down and were hard at it.

Clapping her hands to gain their attention, she perched on a desk at the front, close to the whiteboards, and recapped what she and the chief had discussed.

"That's going to take some doing, pulling all of that off, without getting people flustered, boss," Carla stated with a puzzled brow.

"Yep, I believe you're right. I think it's the way to go. I'm waiting to hear back from the chief, she was contacting the head of Armed Response when I left. Hopefully, he might be able to help us out with a suitable location."

"That should be the least of our worries. My biggest concern is getting hold of the rest of the jury and trying to persuade them to allow us to protect them."

"May I ask why?" Sara asked her partner.

"All right, maybe I wasn't clear enough. How far do we go? If we arrange for the rest of the group to come in, won't they be worried about what's likely to happen to their families? Do we extend the protection to their nearest and dearest?"

Sara tutted. "You're right to be anxious, it's something I should have contemplated. We should bring their closest family members into the fold. My biggest dilemma is how we round these people up? Are they likely to want to be detained against their will?"

Carla shook her head. "It's hardly against their will, and what's the alternative? For each of them to end up in the mortuary?"

Sara puffed out her cheeks. "You know some of them are going to overreact about the plan while others will dismiss it. We're going to have a devil of a job convincing some of them."

"The more time we spend debating it, the more likely we are to be called out to another murder scene."

Sara raised her finger again. "Hear me out before we jump into action. Our priority should also be doing all we can to track down Barrett's gang members, if they're the ones bumping off the victims."

Carla tutted. "You're right. We're never going to be able to manage all this with a tiny team."

"I agree. Let's see what the chief comes back with first. Craig, delve into the Barrett case for me. See if you can find any names of the gang members and their likely addresses in the system." Sara glanced at Carla and shrugged. "It's a start. Can I have a word in my office?"

Carla frowned and then followed Sara. "Have I done something wrong?"

"Why do you always jump to the wrong conclusion? Take a seat. I have something I need to tell you."

They both sat. Sara shuffled the papers strewn across her desk and placed them in a pile, all the while assessing how she should handle the issue on the tip of her tongue.

"You're beginning to worry me. Just come out and say what you have to say, boss." Carla fidgeted.

"Okay, I've debated about whether to share this with you or not, but I can't hold it in any longer."

"What are you talking about? Oh God, you're not pregnant, are you?"

"No, I'm bloody not." Sara inhaled and let the breath out slowly. "On my way back from the chief's office, I bumped into Des, literally."

"And? Is that surprising? Considering he works in the same building, isn't that bound to happen now and again?"

"Sorry, I'm not making myself very clear here. What I'm trying to say is that he seemed very distant, as if he was distracted. Something major possibly running through his mind."

"Maybe he's dealing with a perplexing case and you caught him contemplating what to do next."

"Possibly. I just wondered if everything was all right between you."

Carla shuffled in her seat. "Of course everything's all right, it couldn't be better. We're having a blast."

Sara held her hands up. "All right, there's no need to bite my head off."

"Are we done here?" Carla's tone had turned spiky.

"Yes."

"Good." Her partner stood and marched out of the room.

Jesus! Now I've put my foot in it and upset her. Me and my big mouth. But I had to say something, my gut is telling me there's more to it. As if I haven't got enough on my plate to worry about. She held her head in her hands and proceeded to feel sorry for herself for the next five minutes until she mentally kicked her own backside. Sara returned to the incident room. Carla glanced up from her computer screen and immediately looked away again. The phone on Sara's desk rang, and she bolted back inside to answer it.

"DI Ramsey."

"It's me," the chief's voice sounded hushed, almost conspiratorial. "I've got everything organised. Come and see me and we'll finalise the plans."

"I'm on my way."

She shot out of the office and passed through the incident room, imitating a tornado on a mission. Mary was waiting by the chief's door and showed her in as soon as she arrived.

During the next twenty minutes, Sara and the chief went over what DCI Price had put in place with her contact at the Armed Response Unit. Everything was coming to plan on paper, all they needed to do now was convince the jurors that they were being gathered together for their own protection.

Sara returned to the incident room with a niggle in her stomach and the beginnings of a headache. After declaring what she and the chief had formulated between them, the team got to work, doing their best to locate the rest of the jurors. Commander Wyatt of the Armed Response Unit showed up a couple of hours later with a minibus.

"We'll round them up and then I'll drive them myself to the church out at Swainshill, it's far enough out of the city not to draw attention."

"Sounds great. There's only one more person we need to contact and then we're set to go."

Wyatt casually peered at his watch and then up at Sara. "Time's getting on."

Sara nodded. "I'm aware of that." It didn't stop her glancing at the clock on the wall. It was already six-fifteen. She needed to call Mark, tell him that she would be working late again, the third night on the trot. *Let's hope he's in an accepting frame of mind.*

Drifting into her office, she walked past the window and caught sight of Des's car speeding out of the car park. Her stomach stirred nervously, and Sara clenched and unclenched her hands to ease the tension tightening her shoulders.

"Are you all right?" Carla surprised her by asking from the doorway.

"Gearing myself up to call home," Sara fibbed.

"He'll be fine. Unless you want me to make the call for you?"

"No, that's the coward's way out. Not sure I've reached that point just yet. How are we doing with tracing the other gang members?"

"So-so. According to the system, a few of them are sitting in prison with Barrett on a lesser charge, so we can knock them off the list."

"We're running out of time. What about the missing juror? Anything yet?"

"Nope. She's still AWOL. Hopefully her disappearance is a coincidence and not connected to the gang."

"Let's hope you're right. I'm just going to ring home, and then we'll assess the finer details for this evening." Her head was pounding. She opened her desk drawer, removed a packet of paracetamol and took a couple with a few sips of the cold coffee lying on her desk.

"Mark, how are you?"

"Good. Are you on your way home? If so, I'll make a start on the dinner."

She gulped and closed her eyes. "Umm… sorry to have to do this to you again… but we're closing in on the culprits, and it's all hands to the pumps this evening."

"It's fine. Sara, you never have to apologise to me for doing your job. You're an exceptional copper. I might not appreciate that at times, but I need to tell you that I will always love you, whether you come home for dinner at night or not."

"You're cute. I love you, too. I haven't even had time to check how Mum has been this afternoon. It's been absolute bedlam around here today, culminating in us rounding people up and transporting them to a safe house, sort of. Anyway, I have to get on with organising the team. The sooner we get it sorted, the quicker I can call it a day and come home."

"Enough said. Go. Stay safe."

"I will. See you later." She ended the call and was tempted to ring the hospital, but everything kicked off. The commotion in the incident room forced her out of the chair. "What's going on?"

"Sorry, I got overexcited," Craig announced. "I've managed to trace two key members of the gang, their address is the same."

"Okay, that's great news. You and Barry shoot over there. Keep your distance, use the least conspicuous car. Keep them under surveillance until you hear from me."

"That'll be my boring Ford then," Barry suggested.

"Whatever. Keep in touch via the radio. We'll let you know how we're progressing with collecting the jurors. I take it there's still no news on the missing woman yet?"

Carla shook her head. "Nope, nothing. She's not at home, and I checked with her work: she had the day off today."

"There's not a lot we can do about that then, except put a car outside her home and await her arrival. Who's up for that?"

Marissa and Christine looked at each other and nodded.

"We don't mind doing it, boss," Marissa volunteered.

"Excellent news. I suggest you get over there now. Barry and Craig, you set off at the same time. Let's get this show on the road, peeps."

Commander Wyatt was sitting in the corner, organising his team via the radio. He gave her the thumbs-up, and they set off.

10

*D*es followed Warren out of the station's car park at a safe distance. He'd been guilty of being too eager to begin with but then he took his foot off the pedal and allowed at least three cars to get between his car and Warren's. During the afternoon, since the incident in the hallway, he'd carried out some digging on Warren Fitch and what he'd found out made his skin crawl. He knew a bent copper when he saw one. *How the heck has he got away with it all these years?*

He'd make sure Fitch didn't get away with anything else, not on his watch. He slowed down when he saw Warren indicate and pull up to the kerb up ahead. Turning off his lights, he watched and waited. It wasn't long before a slim blonde came out of a small terraced house and joined him in the vehicle. They leaned over and gave each other a quick kiss, then Warren drove into the traffic again.

Des maintained his distance as his heart pummelled his chest. Over and over he wondered if he was doing the right thing, following Warren, knowing how dangerous he could be. They travelled the width of the city and drew up outside a couple of semi-detached houses in the White Cross area. Des switched off his lights and slid low into his seat to watch what they were up to. There was no movement from either Warren or his passenger for the next ten minutes. Peering out of the window, Des also noticed another vehicle in the vicinity, with two females in the front. His gaze flicked between the two cars until another car arrived and parked directly outside one of the semis.

Warren's car door opened, and he ran across the street to speak with the woman who got out of the car. She smiled at Warren, but then her smile slipped and she tried to run. Then things escalated quickly. The two women in the other car got out and ran across the road to confront Warren and the woman. Warren latched on to the woman's arm and tried to steer her towards his car. There was a lot of shouting going on, and the woman screamed. Nosey neighbours emerged from the nearby houses.

Warren seemed flustered. Des decided to remain incognito for now. It was then that he recognised the two women: they were from Carla's team. *If I get out now, there will be questions to answer when word gets back to Carla that I was here. Jesus, I'm going to need to see how this pans out. If Warren takes the woman, I'm going to need to follow him...*

One of the officers approached Warren, her hand outstretched, and pleaded with him to let the woman go.

Warren laughed. Suddenly, the passenger flew out of Warren's car. She was carrying a metal bar, threatening the two officers. Warren seized the opportunity to drag his captive towards his vehicle.

The officers tried to placate Warren's partner. She was having none of it. Menacingly, she swung the bar back and forth, closing the gap between her and the two officers—that was until one of the officers produced a Taser and aimed it. She dispatched it, and the passenger fell to the ground, jerking frantically as the surge of volts shot through her skinny body.

Warren tucked the woman into the back seat, thumped her in the face and jumped behind the steering wheel. One of the officers ran into the road, doing her best to prevent him from driving off. He clipped her with the car. *Fuck, I need to help her. No, I can't, what I need to do is stick with Warren.*

He turned the key in the ignition and pulled away from the kerb. Warren had put his foot down up ahead. Des halted the car long enough to yell at the copper on the ground, "Are you all right? I've got to stick with him."

The officer shouted and waved him on, "I'm fine. You go."

He smiled and pressed down hard on the accelerator. A mile or so up the road, Warren drove into a car park, close to a wooded area. Des didn't stop, instead he parked a few hundred yards ahead and ran back to find Warren dragging the woman out of the car. She was screaming. He slapped her face a few times, and she slumped into his arms, unconscious. Warren hitched the woman onto his shoulder and headed towards a path leading into the woods. Des skirted around the unlit edge of the car park and followed them.

A few feet along the footpath, Warren dropped her and stood over the woman. He kicked her in the leg to see if she was awake. There was no response. He withdrew a knife from his pocket and flicked it open. Des reacted swiftly and pounced on Warren. He was stunned; the knife flew out of his grasp and into the undergrowth.

"You? What the fuck? I told you what would happen if you didn't back off."

They scrambled to their feet and Des grinned. "Bring it on, buddy."

Warren charged at him, his head down, aiming for Des's stomach. Des stood his ground, waited until the last moment, and then dodged out of the way. Warren ended up face-first in the dirt, brambles sticking to his clothes. He didn't stay down long. Seconds later, fists clenched, Warren was ready for action.

Des stood, his feet wide apart, ready to take the fucker on, knowing that he had to give it his all or likely wind up dead.

Fists flew in every direction, blow after blow, connecting with the other's head, face and body. Before long it was a bloody mess, but it was also an even match—without added weapons, that was, until Warren landed on the ground after a significant blow from Des and searched the undergrowth for his knife. He jumped to his feet and ran at Des. The knife ripped Des's arm. He cried out but then flew at Warren again. *Shit, I'm no match for him, not without a weapon.*

He tried a previous manoeuvre, to dodge out of the way with each thrust Warren made. The knife pierced his skin, and Des felt his strength waning rapidly. He sank to his knees, defeated.

Warren towered over him, his gaze burrowing into Des's. "I told you to fucking back off, you should have listened."

"Do what you have to do with this warning ringing in your ears, mate. The two female officers got a good look at you back there, and they've also got your bird in custody. Do you really think you're going to get away with this?"

A whack around the head sent Warren tumbling to the ground. He was out for the count. The woman had regained consciousness and taken her revenge. She sank to her knees next to Des and sobbed. He held her in his arms for the briefest of moments.

"You did well. You're safe now. I need to get my cuffs on him." Des removed his cuffs from his belt and secured Warren's hands.

Warren stirred and, sensing he was doomed, tried to scrabble to his feet.

Des kicked out and felled him. "Stay there until I say you can move." He ensured the woman was okay and then yanked Warren onto his feet and marched him back to his car. He instructed the woman to sit in the passenger seat and placed Warren in the rear.

Des drove back to the station. He pulled into the car park as Sara and Carla were coming out of the main entrance. He beeped to gain their attention. They walked towards him. Sara eyed him suspiciously before her gaze drifted to the passenger seat and then the rear of the car.

"What's going on, Des?"

"Meet Tina Parks. I believe two of your officers had her house under surveillance. And they also have this man's associate in custody, at least I hope they have."

"I'm not with you. What man?" Sara peered harder into the rear seat but shook her head, unable to make out who the man was in the evening darkness.

Des opened the back door and yanked Warren out of the vehicle.

"What the fuck? I know you," Sara shouted.

"I overheard a conversation he was having in the gents' loo. He's behind the murders, along with his girlfriend."

Sara prodded Warren in the chest. "You sick bastard. You're going down for this."

"Whatever. You'll never make it stick," Warren spat back.

"We'll see about that." Des gripped his arm and steered Warren towards the main entrance, while Sara and Carla helped the distraught woman out of the car and into the station.

Carla wrapped a blanket around her shoulders and fetched her a cup of coffee.

Sara watched Des take Warren through to the custody sergeant, and once Warren had been booked in and banged up in a cell, Des leaned against the wall and placed his hands on his knees.

She sidled up to him. "While I admire your courage, you should have confided in me when I asked you if there was anything wrong earlier."

Des straightened up and faced her. "I wanted to do things my way. Fitch threatened me. I needed to take him down myself, you know what it's like."

"No, I don't, because I have an exceptional team around me. We had it covered, Des."

"Did you? Four murders in a week. Did you even know where the investigation was heading?"

Sara sighed and shook her head. "We were getting there, slowly. We'd sourced the link between all four victims; granted, we thought it was the rest of the gang carrying out the murders, but the truth would have come out in the end."

"How many more lives would have been lost in the meantime?"

"None. Hopefully, we've got all the jurors being held at a secure location. The only one we were missing was Tina Parks."

Des launched himself off the wall and smiled. "I'm glad it's sorted anyway."

"You mentioned you overheard a conversation between Fitch and someone on the phone. Care to enlighten me as to what it was about?"

"Obviously Carla and I discuss our working days together in the evening. If she hadn't told me about Miles Chaddock, I don't think I would have made the connection. I heard Fitch telling the person on the phone that Miles had been a mistake but they had to move on from that. To my knowledge, Miles is quite an unusual name, so it didn't take me long to figure out what was going on. When I left the loo, Warren was waiting for me in the hallway. He pinned me up against the wall and issued a threat. Warned me that if I told anyone, he'd kill me. I had an excruciating dilemma on my hands but chose not to tell Carla, thinking I could sort the fucker out myself. I did some research on him; he's had several disciplinary warnings in the past. I took a punt he was about to strike again and decided to follow him."

"I saw you take off earlier, wondered what you were up to. Sorry if it crossed my mind that you were up to no good."

"I was." He grinned. "You have exceptional instincts, Sara."

"Some days are better than others. I admit, I've been totally off my game this week."

"If this is you being off your game then Carla is right, she told me from the word go that you're a force to be reckoned with."

"Good to know. I'll take that as a compliment. Right, young man, I'm going to order your girlfriend to take you to A and E to get your wounds seen to, and no arguments."

He winced as he touched his damaged arm. Blood had stained the cuff of his sleeve, and it was also running down the back of his hand.

"Can you spare her? Won't you have a lot to do here?"

"Nothing that can't wait. We're in the process of rounding up the rest of the gang now. We have the jurors tucked safely away for the night. Which reminds me, I have to call the commander, make him aware of what has transpired. Now go and get yourself sorted."

Des nodded. "Okay, you're the boss."

They walked back up the narrow hallway, and Carla appeared at the top. Her gaze flicked between them, her brow creased. "What's going on here? Anything I should be worried about?"

"Not at all." Sara chuckled. "I've ordered your fella to go to the hospital. You go with him, make sure he goes directly there and doesn't pass GO."

They all laughed.

"Are you sure you don't want me to hang around?" Carla asked.

"Nope, we have two suspects in their cells, they can sweat it out until the morning. I have an urgent call to make and then I'm out of here. I'll see you both in the morning. We're going to need to get a statement from you, Des."

"I thought as much. Have a good evening, what's left of it."

Sara thought how unlikely that was going to be with the number of tasks she had to handle before she headed home herself, but there was no way she was going to make Carla stay behind when she had her hero to sort out. She looked up at the stairs, wondering if she would have the energy to make it to the top.

The chief appeared. "Are you coming up?"

She smiled wearily and placed a foot on the bottom step. "I was just summoning up the strength."

Sara joined the chief, and they entered the incident room. Marissa and Christine were at their desks, looking shell-shocked.

"How are you both?" Sara enquired.

Christine tutted. "Marissa was the one hit by the car. I keep telling her to go to hospital, but she's having none of it, boss."

"What's this?" the chief asked. "If you've been hurt in the line of duty, you should go and get checked out, Marissa."

"I'm fine, honestly. Glad we've caught the suspects between us. Des did well, didn't he?"

The chief appeared confused.

"I'll tell you over a cup of coffee. You two get off, we're done here for the night," Sara said.

"I'll get the coffees," Carol replied.

Sara dismissed Marissa and Christine and went into her office. There, she rang the commander to bring him up to date. The chief entered the office at the start of the call and listened intently to what Sara was telling the commander. "Shall we agree to keep the jurors there for the night? We should have the rest of the gang rounded up by the morning. I've got several team members on the case."

"A job well done, Inspector. I'll report back to you first thing."

"Thanks, Commander Wyatt." Sara ended the call and heaved out a large sigh. "You got the gist of that, I take it?"

"I did. Sounds like Des needs to be singled out for extra praise."

"I can't disagree, although he should have confided in either me or Carla. He's been lumbered with some fairly bad injuries."

"Brave all the same. Glad we have him here with us."

"Me, too. Now to the elephant in the room, Warren Fitch has to be the candidate for the year to take the 'Bent Copper Twenty Twenty-Two' title. I hope you're going to throw the book at him."

"I won't, personally, but I'll see to it that he doesn't get away with it. What a bastard. Has he said why he did it?"

"Nope. He's bedded down for the night in a nice cosy cell. I'll grill him in the morning."

"Good for you. You and your team have worked wonders on this investigation, Sara, despite the personal problems knocking on your door."

"I'm not about to try and take the credit for this one, boss, it truly was a mixture of intuitive teamwork and genuine coincidences."

"If you insist. Now I'm ordering you to go home and get some rest."

Sara's mobile rang on the desk beside her. She answered as the chief reached the door. Sara waved, but her boss remained rooted to the spot. "DI Ramsey, how can I help?"

"Hi, this is the ward sister from the Women's Ward at the hospital."

Sara closed her eyes and prepared herself for the worst. "Hi, is something wrong?"

"Your father asked me to call you and your sister; Lesley is on her way to us now."

"Oh no. How long has Mum got?" Her throat clogged up with tears, and her mouth dried up.

"A few hours at the most."

Sara shook her head, and the tears bulged. "I'm on my way." She ended the call and bowed her head. "I'm not ready to say goodbye to her... not yet," she mumbled.

Carol Price tore around the desk to comfort her. "I'm so sorry, Sara. Go, you need to be with your parents. Do you want me to ring Mark, let him know you're on your way there?"

"If you wouldn't mind. I need to go. I'll be in touch soon."

"Take all the time you need to deal with your emotions. Get in touch when you can, you hear me?"

Sara grabbed her coat and handbag off the rack and tore down the stairs and out to her car. There, before she started the engine, she paused, hoping the delay would prevent the cancer from consuming her mother and taking her from them. "Mum, Mum, Mum... you don't deserve to go like this. Riddled with this detestable, debilitating disease. Why? Why now? Why ever? Parents are supposed to be indestructible, aren't they?"

After a few minutes of asking the same futile questions over and over, Sara finally began the short trip to the hospital. Lesley's car was in the car park closest to the main entrance. Sara parked a few spaces beyond it and made her way up to the Women's Ward. At one stage, she stopped, her wobbly legs objecting, refusing to carry her. After admonishing her weary body, urging it to correspond with her wishes, she made it to the ward, did the necessary with her hands and entered.

The first thing she spotted was that the curtain had been drawn around her mother's bed. The two nurses nodded and offered her a sympathetic smile.

"Your mother was awake a few minutes ago," the blonde nurse said. "She'll be so pleased to see you."

"I'm not sure I'm prepared for this. Any tips?" She tried to swallow down the lump blocking her windpipe.

"Just be yourself. Try not to let her see how upset you are."

"Believe me, I'm trying. It's been a long few days, and I'm feeling somewhat overwhelmed at the moment."

"We understand. You're going to need to push your trials and tribulations of your working week aside, at least for now."

The door opened behind her, and within seconds her husband had taken her in his arms. She was an emotional wreck in his warm, welcome embrace.

"It's okay, baby. Everything is going to be all right. Come on, sweetheart, don't let her see you like this."

She backed away and wiped the tears staining her cheeks. "I thought I was stronger than this. I guess I don't know myself as much as I thought I did."

He kissed her on both cheeks and held her face in his hands. "We'll get through this together. Stay strong and summon up that beautiful smile of yours. It'll break your mother's heart to see your tears, darling."

Nodding, she removed a tissue from the box on the counter and blew her nose, then took another to wipe her tears. "I'm ready now. I'm so glad you're here. Sorry I couldn't call you myself."

"There's no need to apologise. I've been expecting the call. I knew something didn't feel right this evening. Misty has sensed something was wrong, too, she hasn't settled either."

"You're both so intuitive. Come on then, let's see how she is." She smiled at the nurses and continued the short journey across the ward to her mother's bed. Drawing the curtain aside, she found her sister and father clinging on to each of her mother's hands. "Hello, all. How are you, Mum?" She groaned inwardly, feeling it was such a bungling question for her to ask.

Her mother released her hand from her husband's and motioned for Sara to come closer. "Hello, love. It's lovely to see you. I wasn't sure if you'd be too busy to come."

"Nothing could prevent me from coming to see you, Mum. How are you doing?"

There was little to no colour in her mother's cheeks. Sara noticed the change in her skin in the few days she'd been in hospital, and her heart broke. She did her utmost to hold it together.

"I'm tired. I suppose it's to be expected."

Sara kissed the back of her mother's hand and released it so that her father could gather it up again in his own. She placed a hand on her father's shoulder and squeezed. He smiled up at her, his eyes glistening under the lights overhead.

"I'm glad you're all here with me. We've come through some tough times together over the years. It's a shame Timothy isn't here with us, silly boy. I'll be sure to kick his backside when I meet up with him on the other side."

Sara stared at her mother, stunned by her sense of humour at this late stage in her life.

Mark was the first to chuckle, then they all followed suit.

"He'd better watch out," Mark warned.

Over the next hour or so, her mother summarised their family's history and what it had personally meant to her. Everyone else kept quiet, except for the laughter and the gasps that emerged as her mother brought up incidents some of them had forgotten over the years. Like the time when Sara and Lesley had brought a calf home from one of the neighbouring farms when they were still at primary school and it left a massive cowpat on her father's immaculate lawn at the front of the house, where even as children they were forbidden to play, in case they damaged it.

And then her mother retold the story of their wedding, with all the missing elements her parents had managed to conveniently forget over the years, such as the fact that there had been three of them who had attended the signing of the register on the wedding day, not just two. Her mother had been two months pregnant with Sara's brother, Timothy. She glanced at her father, his cheeks rosy now through sheer embarrassment.

"Now don't you two girls go ribbing your father about that. We were young and in love and, well, things happen when you least expect them to. He's always been my soulmate. I'm so glad you came into my life the way you did, Stephen."

"How did you meet again?" Sara probed gently.

"You tell them, love. You always retell the story much better than I ever did."

Her father cleared his throat. "I used to help out the local coalman on a Saturday. One day we saw a damsel in distress, and Ray, the man I used to work for, ordered me to lend a hand. Your mother had stepped on a drain cover, and her heel got trapped between the bars. She was dressed up, going to a friend's birthday party, I seem to remember."

Her mother smiled at the memory. "I was. I had my best dress and shoes on that day. All I could think about was the hiding I would get from my father when I got home that night. Stephen came to my rescue. He told me to remove my foot from the shoe and then carried me over to a low wall. I had to sit there until he released my shoe."

"Old Ray was laughing his socks off at this point," her father added.

"He was. He was a sweetheart. An old romantic at heart, wasn't he?" her mother agreed, gazing fondly into her husband's eyes.

"That's right. I'm glad he forced me to assist you that day. You insisted on taking me out to repay the inconvenience."

"What? You little devil, Mum. I can't believe you were the one who asked Dad out on a date first!" Sara sniggered.

Her mother nodded. "I was. It's the best decision I ever made in my life. I got some stick for it from my friends, of course. In those days, it wasn't the done thing to ask a fella out. I'm glad I broke the rules. What an adventure we had after that, Stephen, didn't we?"

"Aye, love. I will always treasure the memories we made and the time we spent together."

Her mother removed her hand from his and reached up to stroke his cheek. It was such a loving gesture, one that touched Sara's heart. She clutched her husband's hand; he squeezed it back. Lesley glanced her way, and her lip trembled with emotion. Sara smiled and blew her a kiss.

Her mother stopped talking, exhausted from her exertions, and rested her head back on the pillow for a few moments. After gathering her breath, she lifted her head again and turned her attention to her daughters. "I want to tell you how proud I am to call you my daughters. You've kept me going over the years, with your little quirks and mannerisms. It breaks my heart to be leaving you so soon, especially you, Lesley, only because I hoped I would have seen you married off by now."

"Sorry to have let you down, Mum," Lesley mumbled.

"Hush now, you haven't. You need to find a lovely young man, one like Mark here. Mark, it's been one of my greatest pleasures, knowing you. I'll be honest with you, I never thought Sara would strike lucky a second time, I always thought Philip was one of a kind, but over the last couple of years, you've proved me wrong. Thank you for taking care of our daughter so well. I can tell that you adore her as much as she does you. Your relationship resembles mine and your father's more than you know, Sara. Always be kind to each other. I know that's hard, especially with your job, but Mark only has your best interests at heart. I'm sorry I won't be around to meet any children you might have in the future."

"Oh, Mum," was all Sara had in her to say as the tears bulged and burnt her eyes.

"Be happy, all of you. When my time comes, I don't want you to mourn my parting, I want you to go on with your lives. And, Stephen, don't be a burden on the girls, they have their own lives to lead."

"But…" her father said, only for her mother to place a finger on his lips to silence him.

"No buts, I want you to promise me that you'll find someone new to share your life with."

Her father nodded. "I will."

Her mother wagged a finger. "You need to do something first."

Her father inclined his head and asked, "What's that?"

"Make sure you provide for the children in your will. Knowing you, you'll probably end up with some gold digger of a widow."

Her father looked mortified at the prospect. "Oh gosh, how will I tell? You won't be here to guide me, my love."

Her mother raised an eyebrow. "Don't you be so sure. I'll always be around. I promise to make myself known when you least expect me."

They all laughed, everyone except for her father, who seemed shocked by her mother's words. "I… I don't know what to say," her father whispered.

"The time is coming for us to part. I will always love you, all of you. I've cherished every moment of every day I've ever spent in your company. You've been my heartbeat most days. Go on and lead healthy and happy lives." She rested her head back and closed her eyes.

Sara watched her mother's chest rise and fall a couple of times and then stop. Mark squeezed her hand tightly, and fresh tears ran down her cheeks. She wanted to speak, to tell her father that her mother had gone, but she struggled to get the words past the large lump blocking her throat.

"Elizabeth?" Her father leaned forward and kissed her mother on the cheek. He turned back to face his daughters and shook his head. "She's gone. My heart and my soul will never be the same again."

Lesley sobbed and covered her mother's hand with tiny kisses. "You'll always be in our hearts, Mum."

Sara released Mark's hand and hugged her father and then her sister. "She will never be far away from us."

Mark left and returned a little while later with the blonde nurse. She checked her mother's vital signs and nodded, confirming their mother's departure from this world.

EPILOGUE

"*W*here has this week gone?" Sara complained.

"There's been a lot to organise." Mark came up behind her and wrapped his arms around her waist.

"We managed it, between us. It means we can now send Mum on her way and not worry if we did things right or not."

"She would have loved what we've arranged."

"We couldn't have done this without your help, Mark. You've stepped up to the plate and taken over when things ended up being too tough for us all. I'll forever be in your debt."

"Nonsense. I loved your mother as if she were my own. This was all a parting gift for her."

"Talking of which, we'd better go. Dad will be getting anxious if we're not there at least thirty minutes before we have to set off for the church."

"What are we waiting for then?"

They shared a kiss, and Sara saw to Misty's needs. She then slipped her feet into her black court shoes, and Mark helped her on with her 'funeral coat' as she referred to it.

Over the past week, they had made the arrangements together, as a family, but when things had overwhelmed them, Mark had swooped in and picked up the slack to pull everything together in time. Sara had taken the week off work, at the chief's insistence, however, she'd been in daily contact with Carla and the team, regarding what was going on with the investigations.

Warren Fitch had asked for a plea bargain, in exchange for a lesser sentence if he spilled the beans. Between the chief, Sara and Carla, they had all agreed that wasn't on the cards. The Crown Prosecution Service wholeheartedly agreed with them as the evidence spoke for itself against Fitch and his girlfriend. Lorraine and her team had managed to find a minute amount of trace elements on the bike, and there was also blood from a couple of the victims on the metal weapons they had used.

Tina Parks had agreed to reveal what she'd been subjected to on the stand when the case eventually got to court.

In the end, with the odds stacked against him, Fitch had crumbled and admitted that Roger Barrett had, metaphorically speaking, held a gun to his head for years. He'd been bent for over ten years, stealing evidence, changing reports on the system and roughing up witnesses on the villain's behalf. Now there was no way back for him, and he knew that.

His girlfriend had also disclosed all, when Carla had interviewed her under caution.

They were both going down for very long stretches, if they survived. Gangs as large as Barrett's had no end of criminals they could count on to kill someone. Which meant that Fitch and Mona would spend the rest of their lives nervously looking over their shoulders.

Sara and Mark arrived at her parents' house. A lump formed in her throat the second she laid eyes on her mother's coffin, lying in the back of the horse-drawn hearse. This had been one of Mark's most welcome ideas. The church was only up the road, it made sense for all of them to walk alongside the coffin, to celebrate her mother's final farewell.

Lesley was standing next to her father in the kitchen. She hugged them both. They all wiped the tears from their eyes.

"Your mother would want us to be resilient today," her father said. "Let's not let her down, eh? She's out of pain now, that's all that matters. Life goes on, girls, life goes on. Maybe not for the better, but it still goes on."

"How are you holding up, Dad?" Sara asked.

"I've surprised myself. I'm much better than I ever thought I would be. She was right, you know, she's still around us. I get a waft of her perfume every night after I switch the light off in the bedroom."

"That must be such a great comfort to you, Dad," Lesley said.

"It is. Now, girls, let's get to the church. I think your mother is looking forward to the ride. It was her greatest wish to have a horse-drawn carriage for our wedding, but we simply didn't have the funds back then. Thank you, Mark, for arranging such a wonderful exit for her."

Mark shook her father's hand. "It was a pleasure, sir."

The undertaker appeared in the doorway. "We're all set to go, but only if you're ready."

Sara smiled. "We're ready, aren't we?"

Everyone nodded. Lesley linked arms with her father, and Sara clutched her husband's hand as they followed the undertaker out of the house.

It was a magical experience to be a part of. All the village turned out to show their respects to their wonderful mother.

After the beautiful service and her father's emotional eulogy to the love of his life, they assembled at the graveside. Her mother's coffin was laid to rest beside her own mother and father.

Sara picked up a red and a white rose from the silver tray offered to her by the local vicar and took a few steps towards the grave. She threw the flowers on top of the coffin and whispered, "You were the best mum any of us could have wished for. A piece of my heart goes with you, beautiful lady. May you watch over us, until we meet again."

She turned, walked back to Mark and clung to his arm.

"I love you," he whispered.

Sara gazed up at him. "Thank you for being a part of my special family."

THE END

*T*hank you for reading the fifteenth book in the DI Sara Ramsey series. Sara and her intrepid team will back in **Crossing The Line** yet another serial killer thriller, now available.

*U*ntil then, maybe you'd also like to try one of my edge-of-your-seat thriller series. Grab the first book in the best-selling Justice here, **Cruel Justice**

Or the first book in the spin-off Justice Again series, **Gone in Seconds.**

*M*aybe you'd enjoy a series set in the beautiful Lake District, the first book in the DI Sam Cobbs is now available, pick up your copy of **To Die For** here.

*P*erhaps you'd prefer to try one of my other police procedural series, the DI Kayli Bright series here, **The Missing Children.**

*O*r maybe you'd enjoy the DI Sally Parker series set in Norfolk, UK. **WRONG PLACE.**

*T*he first book in the gritty HERO series can be found here. **TORN APART**

. . .

r why not try my first psychological thriller here. **I Know The Truth**

KEEP UP WITH M A COMLEY ON SOCIAL MEDIA HERE.

Pick up a FREE Justice novella by signing up to my newsletter today.
https://BookHip.com/WBRTGW

BookBub
www.bookbub.com/authors/m-a-comley

Blog
http://melcomley.blogspot.com

Why not join my special Facebook group to take part in monthly giveaways.

Readers' Group

Or follow me on TikTok

Printed in Great Britain
by Amazon

15979811R00108